a dare maid in vain

A REGENCY ROMANCE

TRISHA FUENTES

A Dare Maid in Vain
A Regency Romance
Copyright © 2024 by Trisha Fuentes
All rights reserved.

Book Cover and formatting provided by Trisha Fuentes
https://bit.ly/m/trishafuentes

No part of this book may be reproduced in any form or by any electronic or mechanical means, including information storage and retrieval systems, without written permission from the author, except for the use of brief quotations in a book review.

ISBN: 979-8-3303-4330-0 (Paperback)

Published by
Ardent Artist Books
www.ardentartistbooks.com

about ardent artist books

➡ ABOUT US

Ardent Artist Books was established in 2008

We publish modern and historical romances once a month!

Get Your FREE List: Published & Upcoming Books
visit our website at:
https://bit.ly/3Wva4o0

➡ WE HAVE BOOK TRAILERS TOO!

Follow us on YouTube!
https://bit.ly/3W3xn7a

Like, Subscribe & Comment

➡ READ SERIALIZED FICTION!

Visit our website today to download one of our stories that unfold in bite-sized pieces!

Each installment is just 99¢!

https://bit.ly/3LsDpJL

➡ LET'S CONNECT!

Fuel your love of fiction with exclusive content and captivating insights from Ardent Artist Books. Whether you crave the thrill of modern narratives or the timeless elegance of historical fiction, our newsletter delivers a curated selection straight to your inbox. Plus, as a welcome gift, receive a FREE downloadable eBook:

"The Family Fix"

https://bit.ly/49BR3UB

contents

1. The Daring Bet	1
2. A Chaotic Soirée	13
3. A Reckless Scheme	25
4. Morning Calm	35
5. A London Garden	41
6. Mistaken Intentions	47
7. The Abduction	57
8. Revelations on the Road	67
9. The Arrival at Woodfeld Estate	83
10. The Morning After	95
11. The Ton's Response	105
12. Secret Longing	117
13. Confessions	127
14. Departure from London	137
Epilogue	149

YOU MIGHT ALSO LIKE...

The Surprise Heir	165
One Starry Night	167
Service Daughter Series	169
About Trisha	173
Also by Trisha Fuentes	175

CHAPTER ONE
the daring bet
LONDON, ENGLAND, 1814

London shimmered under a brilliant sky, the air alive with the pulsating heartbeat of The Season. The streets bustled with elegantly dressed gentlemen and ladies, their laughter echoing through the vibrant thoroughfares as carriages rolled by, the polished wheels gliding over cobblestones with effortless grace. Flower stalls overflowed with blooms in every hue, competing with the enticing scent of pastries wafting from nearby bakeries. At the heart of this bustling metropolis, the opulent mansions of Mayfair stood proud, each more splendid than the last, twinkling chandeliers reflecting the day's excitement.

In one such mansion, the sun poured through open windows, illuminating a gathering of society's finest. Ladies adorned in pastel gowns fluttered about like butterflies, while gentlemen engaged in spirited conversations punctuated by laughter. The clinking of fine china intermingled with the soft strains of a string quartet, creating an atmosphere of delightful exuberance.

At the center of this fashionable tea gathering, Lady Emily Percy held court among her friends. Her golden curls, artfully arranged, framed a face that radiated warmth and elegance, a striking contrast to her delicate gown of soft lavender that highlighted her statuesque figure without betraying the slightest hint of excess.

Lady Emily handed her shawl over to Miss Connelly, her lady's maid.

Without knowing, Miss Connelly was suddenly under inspection...

"Do tell us, my dear, how one manages to look dazzling whilst doing the laundry," teased her friend, Miss Beatrice Caldwell, a flirtatious debutante known for her relentless pursuit of suitors. Beatrice's sapphire eyes sparkled with mischief as she lounged against a chaise, her bright pink dress complementing the ensemble.

Emily chuckled, her laughter ringing like chimes. "If only my maid would divulge her secrets! The last I checked, 'water and soap' did not support my beauty regimen!"

Laughter erupted around them, and the banter flowed effortlessly. Marianne curtsied to the gentry and made her leave.

Lord Jasper Fairmont, a witty gentleman with the uncanny ability to weave humor into any conversation, leaned forward, his grin infectious. "Perhaps you ought to take a page from our friend Edward, Lady Emily. Rumor has it he usually looks quite stunning. Why, he even manages to spark gossip without lifting a finger!"

Emily enjoyed the friendly banter, feeling a warmth in her chest. But beneath the polished exterior and laughter, she felt restless. Even this glamorous party couldn't satisfy her longing for something new.

"Do you suppose he truly holds any interest in our dear Lady

Percy?" Beatrice asked, her voice laced with glee. "Scandalous as it sounds, an elopement would certainly shake things up!"

"The idea is positively ludicrous!" Lady Emily said, shaking her head, though her eyes glimmered with intrigue.

"Is it ludicrous or is it simply... daring?" chimed in another voice, Miss Lavinia Whitcomb, a vivacious friend whose keen sense of adventure often landed her at the center of tempting escapades. "Just imagine! To steal away from this wretched tedium and dance along the path of *scandal*!"

A ripple of excitement coursed through their group. "But dear Emily, it might do you good to enliven the evening," Jasper suggested playfully. "What's a little scandal, after all, when the thrill of unexpected romance awaits?"

With each playful proposal, Lady Emily's heart raced a beat too fast. She could picture it now: a clandestine midnight elopement with Lord Edward Grey, the notorious rake whose very name conjured both admiration and foreboding among their circles.

"Perhaps a wager would spark your adventurous spirit!" Lavinia laughed, eyes alight with mischief. "We propose you carry out this preposterous act. A scandalous elopement with the Earl of Grey before the Season's end!"

The notion landed like a delightful little snowball, gathering momentum as Beatrice, Jasper, and Lavinia volleyed playful suggestions back and forth.

"Only if you do this without drawing attention—imagine the suspense! You must procure a place to meet without any of us being astutely aware. I imagine it's all rather exhilarating, don't you think?" Jasper's smirk widened.

Emily's mind whirled as excitement battled with the weight of decorum. "You jest! The consequences would be appalling! My family would—"

"Ah, judge not the folly of youth!" another voice interjected, Miss Arabella, the sensible one, leaning in closer. "What better adventure to guarantee your story will be the talk of every salon? As long as you keep your wits about you!"

"But to elope?" Lady Emily's heart beat faster at the mere notion, piqued by the absurdity yet frightened by its implications.

As laughter swelled and her friends rallied around the challenge, she felt herself slipping into their enthusiasm. Her eyes sparkled as she leaned forward, her heart igniting with possibilities. "Very well, I shall entertain this madness! Why shouldn't I be daring? After all, things must change!"

"Splendid! We must decide the terms, the rules—everything!" cheered Beatrice, leaning forward animatedly.

MISS CONNELLY, Lady Emily's astute lady's maid, had been listening from a discreet corner, her expression a curious blend of amusement and unease. She adored Lady Emily's spirited nature, yet a pang of caution tugged at her heartstrings. The room was electric with excitement as the young ladies concocted plans, but Marianne couldn't help but contemplate the ramifications of such reckless antics.

What if something went amiss? Her own upbringing, though humble, had instilled in her a healthy respect for consequence. This was one challenge that spiraled into unfamiliar terrain. Even as she smiled at Lady Emily's enthusiasm, a seed of worry unfurled deep in her chest. Lady Emily craved adventure, a longing that echoed in her very soul. Yet, the chasm between their respective stations threatened to widen with every daring notion tossed into the air.

"Is this truly wise, my lady?" Marianne ventured discreetly, but Lady Emily merely flashed her an impish grin.

"Ah, Miss Marianne! Why waste this perfect moment for adventure? Rally behind me, for today, holds promise!"

The enthusiasm was contagious as Lady Emily solemnly accepted. Her friends raised their teacups, the clink resonating through the plush room, a toast to the absurdity of the bet.

"To adventure, mischief, and a bit of scandal!" they chimed in unison, laughter spilling into the air like confetti.

As they toasted, a silent pact forged among them lit a bond of excitement laced with secrecy. Amidst the drumming of her heart and the warmth of their shared bravado, Emily's gaze drifted towards the window. Beyond the opulence lay the bustling streets of London, teeming with life, energy, and a hint of freedom—waiting just for her.

"Oh, Miss Marianne, do perk up," she exclaimed, glancing back at her lady's maid, a mask of resolve softening her playful demeanor as she considered the possibility of taking the leap. This was her moment to alter the course of her life. Resolute yet barely comprehending the risks at stake, she glanced back at Marianne, their eyes locking for a brief, startling moment of understanding.

Perhaps they would change the molehills of their lives into mountains of adventure.

As the clamor of excitement surged around her, she held her breath, her thoughts drifting towards the evening ahead, a soirée where daring plans would take a tangible form. The stakes had been raised, and with every sip of tea, every whisper and laughter, her heart echoed the promise of the unknown that lay ahead.

With the laughter of her lady and her friends still shimmering in the air, Miss Connelly slipped away from the lively gathering, her heart a mixture of concern and anticipation. She navigated the opulent halls of the Percy residence, pausing only briefly to glance over her shoulder as she departed the brightly lit drawing room. The echoes of spirited chatter faded behind her, replaced by the subtle hush of the house.

Her feet moved quietly across the polished floor, leading her deftly down a set of narrow stairs toward the servant's quarters. The heavy air of the main floor, filled with layers of chatter and the clinking of tea china, fell away as she descended. The aroma of baked goods and fresh bread growing stronger, mingled with the damp scent of the kitchen, filled her lungs and comforted her in a way she could not fully articulate.

Reaching the door to the kitchens, she pushed it open to enter a world quite distinct from the dainty elegance of where her lady resided. Here, the hustle of servants in white aprons filled the room, bustling about as they arranged dishes on counters or stoked the large oven with hissing coals. The air was warmer, and a gentle buzz of voices filled the space, weaving together in an affectionate symphony of familial camaraderie.

"Miss Connelly!" A voice chimed from across the kitchen, and Marianne turned to see Mrs. Hutchins, the head housekeeper, bustling toward her with a look that mixed warmth and authority. "You're looking a bit peaky, dear. Have you taken a moment to eat?"

Marianne shook her head. "I have not, ma'am. I was just thinking a cup of tea would do me well, if that's alright."

"Oh, it is quite alright," Mrs. Hutchins replied, a smile spreading across her face. "Lord knows how our young ladies can talk the ears off of any bystander! Come now, let me fetch you a piping hot cup."

As Mrs. Hutchins went to the wide table where the remnants of the day's tea service remained, Marianne approached the buffet, glancing over the spread. Arrayed beautifully, it showcased the culinary talents of the kitchen staff: delicate pastries adorned with icing, a selection of fruits, and crusty rolls, all ready for the evening's small indulgences.

Yet, as she reached to grab a bun, a flicker of guilt sparked in her chest. As Lady Emily's maid, Marianne felt the weight of an unspoken rule wrapped around her; she could not partake in the lavish offerings of the family she served. These delicacies were for the guests, of whom she considered herself nothing but a shadow —always present in the background, tasked with ensuring the success of the evening without a thought to her needs.

Before returning to her thoughts too deeply, she turned to find herself surrounded by soft laughter, the hearty banter filling the room with homely comfort. She caught sight of a few fellow maids and footmen, each hard at work but no less engaging in their convivial exchanges. Their faces brightened at her arrival, and for once, she relaxed in her station, as camaraderie filled the kitchen.

"Look who decided to grace us with her presence!" exclaimed Mary, another lady's maid who worked under the employ of the Percys, her cheeks flushed with joy. "Fancy a morsel, Marianne? You'd best gather some before the others discover your absence."

Footmen stationed near the doorway leaned in with cheeky grins. One among them, a tall, broad-shouldered lad named Thomas, stroked his chin, eyeing her with a playful glint in his eye. "Are you quite certain you've time to chat, Connelly? One can only wonder how long Lady Emily'll manage without her finest lady maid!"

"Oh, stop feigning concern, Thomas. You are only after the chance to distract her from work," Mary teased, ripping a pastry into pieces with a flourish. "As if she'd ever leave you in charge of anything important!"

Marianne's heart fluttered, slightly amused yet cautious. It had been some time since her beauty had garnered the attention of a man, especially one like Thomas, whose sunny charm made her laugh as easily as it pulled warmth from her cheeks. Flirting, though, was a dance she had circled around without stepping onto the floor.

"Stop it," she protested lightheartedly, a tilt of her head as she attempted to ignore the blush creeping up her neck. "I assure you, my work shall never suffer because of such theatrics."

"Ah, but your company shall!" Thomas declared with mock dismay, crossing his arms over his chest as he leaned against the doorframe. "How can we ensure your health if you continue to hide away, working tirelessly for our oblivious young ladies?"

"Maybe not hide away, but perhaps guard our gluttonous spirits." Another footman, a wirier fellow named George, chimed in, expertly lifting a pastry from the buffet and offering it to Marianne with a wink. "Wouldn't want to see you fade away, outshone by delightfully fat surges of cream and buttery crusts!"

She accepted the pastry with a playful roll of her eyes, feeling uncharacteristically lighthearted at the banter that surrounded her, their whispers and laughter creating an ephemeral bubble of warmth and camaraderie. "Oh, you don't need to worry about me; I assure you that I am quite hearty. The diet of dusted sauces and herbal tones will fill me quite nicely! But one might say that tea is a fine companion for sustenance!"

As Mrs. Hutchins returned with her tea, the group erupted into a pliable rhythm of conversation. They shared stories of mischievous happenings that had spilled into other households, and spontaneous decisions that resulted in ankle-deep mud during spring rains. Laughter erupted as they replayed the day's happenings and the occasional absurdity of their lives in service.

The evening light cast a golden hue through the kitchen window, a warm embrace as the friendships blossomed around her. Here among the whirl and bustle, she felt a natural ease, a sense of belonging that transcended her position. The chains of social convention loosened amidst the laughter and everyday struggles —she was not merely a maid disguised among the gilded trappings of the upper class, but a sister among others who shared her burdens and desires.

As the cheerful chaos continued, Marianne stole a glance at Mrs. Hutchins, who wore an expression of quiet pride, managing the kitchen with a skilled touch that brought harmony to the bustling activities. In her own way, the head housekeeper ruled this domain, forging connections that felt as warm as the hearth where the tea was steeping, inspiring a loyal camaraderie among the servants.

Feeling emboldened amidst their playful provocations, Marianne found herself drawn in, laughing more freely, even retorting playfully when spurred on by Thomas, who rallied his friends to excel at charming her with encourageable antics.

Oh, how different this felt from the decorum of the drawing room! Her heart soared, and the burden of worry for Lady Emily's outlandish plans receded, if only for a moment. Here in the kitchen, she was not merely a fleeting specter in a waltz. She was one with them, a heartbeat among many. Perhaps it was spirited, perhaps whimsical, but it lent her strength enough to step back into the evening, bolstered by this renewed sense of place and belonging.

CHAPTER TWO
a chaotic soirée

The grand Mayfair mansion thrummed with electric energy, an opulent jewel nestled amidst the vibrant pulse of London during The Season. Lush draperies adorned the sweeping staircase, flowing like waterfalls from the banister toward polished marble floors. Every window bloomed with arrangements of fragrant roses and peonies, their petals swaying gently in the balmy evening air. Inside, the low hum of laughter and the cheerful clinking of tea sets mingled with the dulcet strains of a string quartet, their music wafting through the hallways like a sweet breeze.

As carriages began to glide up the cobbled street, the light from chandeliers danced across the polished wood floors, illuminating the excited faces of guests taking their places. All around, the elite of society gathered, dressed in their fineries, sparkling jewels adorning elegant gowns and waistcoats tailored to perfection. It was a soirée replete with anticipation.

Lady Emily Percy entered the ballroom with her companion, Miss Connelly at her side, turning heads with the grace of a gazelle. Radiant in a gown of soft lavender that accentuated the delicate curve of her waist, her golden curls cascaded down her back, catching the light in a halo-like glow. Onlookers barely managed to mask their admiration as she offered them warm smiles, sweeping through the crowd with charming ease. Her presence created a ripple effect, sparking quiet whispers of envy among the women and fleeting admiration from the men.

"Look at her," one lady whispered to her companion, casting a green-eyed glance Emily's way. "It's as if the flowers bloom only for her."

"Quite so," her friend responded, her own tone laced with thinly veiled scorn. "And yet, how dull she seems, forever lacking a suitor."

Meanwhile, Miss Connelly followed closely, a bemused smile playing on her lips as she took in the spectacle. Though trained to remain unobtrusive in her role as lady's maid, she keenly observed every flicker of emotion, every subtle shift in the room's atmosphere. There was amusement in Lady Emily's interactions, but lurking beneath the surface was the tension of whispered rivalries, darting glances, and unspoken judgments.

"Bloated with their own importance, they are," Marianne murmured under her breath, her hazel eyes scanning the gathering. "And yet, they seem utterly enchanted by your charm, my Lady."

"Why, Miss Connelly! You know full well that a little charm goes a long way." Lady Emily laughed, the sound warm and rich, drawing attention to her as she waved excitedly at familiar faces. "Now, go upstairs with the rest of the lady's maids."

Marianne glanced up toward the rafters, a few other maids were clustered upstairs and she made her way towards the stairs.

Amid the mingling crowds, several prominent gentlemen erupted into cheerful fits of laughter, eager to catch Lady Emily's eye or to make their mark with grand displays of charm. They jostled for position, vying for her attention as if she were the most coveted prize of the evening. But amid the suitors, one presence commanded more than just attention—Lord Edward Grey. The very mention of his name sent ripples through the ballroom.

He strolled in, all rakish charm and easy confidence, a devil-may-care smile gracing his lips. Eyes twinkled mischievously—his reputation preceded him, igniting a blend of admiration and scandal amongst the guests.

The balcony overlooking the ballroom offered a rare moment of reprieve from the chaos below. Miss Connelly stepped outside, relief flooding her as the cool evening air danced against her skin. She inhaled deeply, savoring the fragrant blossoms that clung to the wrought-iron trellis, offering a moment's distraction from the swirling sea of aristocrats within.

"Marianne! Come join us!" a familiar voice called. She turned to see two other ladies' maids, Jane and Clara, perched at the edge of the banister. Their skirts brushed the polished wood, and the excitement in their eyes mirrored the enchantment of the gathering inside.

With a wave of her hand, Marianne approached, a smile stretching across her face. "Too often, I find myself trapped amid the extravagant antics of high society. A respite is welcome indeed."

Jane, a spirited young woman with auburn hair pinned in soft curls, leaned conspiratorially closer. "Any respite from that dull thrum—particularly amongst the likes of them!" She gestured broadly toward the ballroom atmosphere, though her piercing gaze lingered where the guests jostled for a position below.

Clara, quieter and more precocious, peered over the edge, her hazel eyes widening. "I declare, look who looms among them! None other than the Earl of Grey himself. How utterly dashing he is this evening!" Her voice barely contained her breathless admiration.

Marianne followed their gaze, settling her eyes upon the renowned rake. He stood there, disarming and charismatic, his tousled dark hair framing a chiseled jawline that could make even the most stoic of hearts flutter. The way he interacted with the crowd—a disarming charm combined with an aura of danger—captured her fascination. As he leaned closer to an elegantly dressed lady, eyes sparkling with mirth, laughter erupted from the surrounding group.

"Must you chatter so? You two are positively besotted," Marianne teased, her tone laced with mockery even as she succumbed to her curiosity. She leaned over the banister, joining them in assessing the scene.

"Can you blame us?" Jane practically swooned, her eyes alight as they absorbed the spectacle of the notorious rake. "He's everything a woman could hope for—handsome, mysterious, and utterly unattainable!"

"Utterly unattainable indeed," Marianne replied, her voice lilting with a hint of sarcasm, but she could not deny the thrill that shot through her at the sight of him. Despite her efforts to remain unaffected, some part of her couldn't help but admire the way he navigated the throng of guests, his laughter ringing through the air.

"He does seem to enjoy the attention," Clara noted, captivated. "Do you think he will dance with Lady Emily tonight?"

A sharply drawn breath passed through Marianne, her heart fluttering momentarily at the thought. "If there is any sensibility in that man," she murmured, glancing toward her lady in the ballroom below, "then I imagine he will be drawn to her like a moth to a flame." The truth, however, was more layered—a thick mix of admiration and concern for Lady Emily, who yearned for something more than the constraints of their world.

"Let us hope your lady catches his eye. He's the sort who might actually dangle a hint of real adventure, rather than the customary chit-chat!" Jane leaned closer, eyes sparkling with mischief.

"I sincerely doubt she'd have much interest in the adventure he does offer," Marianne remarked, part playful, part serious. "He's not merely the talk of the town for his charm. There are always whispers—followed by ladies left despondent."

"Better a fleeting romance than none at all!" Clara quipped back, a teasing smile stretching across her face. "What do we live for if not to partake in some delightful scandal?"

"Ladies, I dare say that your ideas are far too extravagant." Marianne could not repress a grin. "Yet I cannot deny the temptation of mischief."

"I can hear your heartbeat quickening at merely the thought!" Jane laughed, nudging Marianne playfully. "You'd make an excitable suitor, were you one to sway your lady's attention toward him."

Suddenly, the laughter of the gathering below reached a frenetic pitch. Lord Grey's voice rang through the air, low and inviting, as he leaned in closer to a lady wearing sapphire satin. Her laughter was airy, yet Marianne could see the tension in the others, ready to react should he decide to shift his gaze.

With her heart racing, cocooned by the light banter, Marianne briefly abandoned her reservations, swept into the chaos of genuine excitement surrounding Edward Grey's presence. "Let us merely watch," she suggested, a sense of camaraderie uniting them all in their curiosity. "If nothing else, it will be amusing."

A moment of shared silence descended as they surveyed the Lord, captured by his devilish good looks and sophisticated aura. Jane sighed, her expression knotting with dreamy helplessness. Clara, however, leaned closer to Marianne, a conspiratorial grin illuminating her features.

"Imagine what it would be like to accompany him to a ball. Dancing with him," Clara imagined aloud, fluttering her lashes dramatically. "An adventure in and of itself, several scandalous moments wrapped in one."

The trio erupted into laughter, glancing back towards the ballroom, where the mood gathered another layer of tension as pairs twirled across the floor, blissfully blind to the brewing mischief surrounding them on the balcony. Marianne caught sight of Lady Emily, light as a feather, moving through like a dream, her elegance unmistakable even in the dizzying throng.

In that moment, enveloped in laughter with her fellow maids, Marianne could not quell the excitement that coursed through her veins. This spirited notion of adventure, against all judgment, ignited something within her; an idea danced, half-formed at the back of her mind. They must discover the world behind the walls of privilege, unearthing where true detours awaited them.

As Lord Grey stirred the yet-simmering air with charisma and charm, Marianne felt the weight of expectation shift ever so slightly. She stole one last glance towards her lady, delighting in her radiant laughter that mingled with the music blaring from within, uncertain of what lay ahead but ever eager to witness the ensuing excitement.

"Does he ever hold a single thought for propriety?" Marianne whispered, an eyebrow raised, as she caught sight of Lord Grey's typical theatrics as he placed an exaggerated hand on his heart in response to a young lady's compliment.

"Not when he has audiences such as this," Jane replied, suppressing a giggle.

Marianne then saw Lord Grey walk straight toward Lady Emily and her heart raced with anticipation. *Let the games begin...*

"LADY EMILY... I dare say, you radiate more than the chandelier this evening," Lord Edward observed, a glimmer of mischief dancing in his emerald eyes as he approached her with casual aplomb.

"Why, my Lord, such flattery," Lady Emily playfully arched an eyebrow, accepting the compliment with a graceful tilt of her head. "Is this a strategy to distract me from your own shortcomings?"

"O, but yes! Such an astute observer you are." He feigned a sigh of mock despair. "What would I do without your keenness?"

As the evening unfolded, the gathering grew more spirited, with every corner filled with candor and camaraderie. In one group, ladies teased their gentlemen about their presumed talents, while the men retorted with ludicrous stories of their adventures in distant lands. Witty banter echoed through the ballroom, drawing amused glances from unassuming spectators.

"Should we not have a contest?" one gentleman, emboldened by drink and laughter, proposed. "A test of our charms to see who can impress the ladies most by evening's end!"

The suggestion sent shockwaves of laughter rippling through the assembly, igniting an enthusiastic uproar.

"To each suitor, we shall assign a lady, and you must do your utmost to win her favor!" someone chimed in, wobbling slightly as they tried to regain their balance amid the raucous hilarity. The room erupted into cheers and even playful jeers, all unaware of how chaotic the ensuing competition would become.

Amidst the revelry, Lord Edward flashed an impish grin and turned his attention back to Lady Emily, captivated by her effervescent spirit.

"Naturally, I shall win this contest," he boasted, leaning slightly closer, his voice low, letting the humming crowd fade momentarily. "There exists no lady whose favor I cannot win."

"And what of the competition?" Lady Emily quipped back, her eyes sparkling with intrigue.

At that precise moment, her teasing was interrupted as a commotion broke out behind them. A series of half-hearted attempts at exaggerated flirtation and comedic tales tumbled forth from other suitors, ushering in a veil of mirth that further distracted the guests.

Suddenly, as the delightful chaos swirled through the hall, Lord Grey swept Lady Emily's hand into his own, his eyes eluding any seriousness. "Care to dance, my Lady? It seems this soirée could use a touch of true artistry and wit to elevate it above the chaos."

Marianne, observing the two from up above, felt the tinges of concern begin to weave through her thoughts. She found herself entertained but cautious, aware of the dance's electric chemistry and the lighthearted flirting that echoed something deeper lurking beneath the surface.

As they glided across the floor, Edward charmed Emily with effortlessly clever quips, drawing joyful laughter from her.

"You know," he began, a glint of mischief teasing the corners of his mouth, "should you wish for a more thrilling experience than this soirée provides, I could be persuaded to help you find an escape through the back door."

Lady Emily leaned in closer, her voice barely above a whisper, rich with jesting intrigue. "Perhaps I am in search of something a touch more scandalous?"

Her playful banter caused strands of laughter to ripple from nearby guests—ones that stoked the fire of adventure blooming within her heart, blissfully unaware of the implications weaving around her words.

Marianne's heart raced. *What have you done?* she thought, her instincts kicking into high gear amidst the jubilant chaos enveloping them. Ominous thoughts festered as she observed the merriment around her, but just as soon they were whisked away, supplanted by laughter and intriguing distractions regarding elopements—a hot topic that swept through the gathering like wildfire.

As Lady Emily danced among the swirling masses, her laughter rang like chimes against the gilded walls of the grand ballroom, while Marianne stood alone by pillar up above.

She observed Lord Grey, that notorious rake, effortlessly ensnaring the attention of other ladies with his roguish charm and disarming grin. Each flirtatious glance and whispered jest seemed deliberate, a carefully orchestrated performance tailored to captivate yet another audience of naive admirers. His dark hair tousled just so, he leaned in dramatically to a particularly giggly debutante, making her blush as she clutched her lace fan to her cheeks in delight. Marianne's stomach churned, a tightening knot of trepidation twisting within her. She could not shake the nagging worry that beneath the semblance of playful banter lurked a man far less innocent than he allowed himself to appear. *How could Lady Emily want to marry him when his nature is to deceive?*

Marianne's gaze sharpened, taking in the animated flurry of silks and laughter, now cluttered with the encroaching specter of scandal. Lord Grey's charm radiated across the room, drawing captivated glances from every corner while Lady Emily, capable and enchanting, remained blissfully unaware of the precarious balance she danced upon. The audacity of his flirtation with the other ladies made Marianne's breath quicken; *what would become of Lady Emily's reputation should a whisper of his interest in her reach their troublesome peers?* Such a connection would generate countless whispers, raising eyebrows and unfurling the kind of gossip that could tumble like a wayward snowball, altering the course of a lady's future with alarming speed. *No*—Marianne bitterly thought—*it could not happen.* That handsome devil with the emerald eyes could easily charm the façade off a statue, and Marianne shuddered at the thought of Lady Emily falling into his careless allure, her dreams of adventure shadowed by the very real concerns of propriety. One reckless dalliance had the potential to engulf them both in social ruin, and she resolved, in that moment, to keep a close watch.

CHAPTER THREE
a reckless scheme

The aftermath of the soirée filled the air with an electric silence as Lady Emily and Marianne settled into the dimly lit carriage that glided through the quiet streets of London. The clatter of horse hooves echoed softly against the cobblestones, a distant reminder of the vibrant revelry they had left behind. Gilded streetlamps flickered like tiny stars above them, illuminating the intricate details of the passing manors, now shrouded in night. The captivating energy of the evening slowly faded, yet excitement danced in Lady Emily's eyes.

Inside the carriage, Lady Emily radiated an effervescent enthusiasm. Her cheeks flushed with the thrill of the soirée, she leaned closer to Marianne, her voice a hushed whisper of enthusiasm.

"Did you see how Lord Grey looked at me?" Her laughter mingled with the creaking of the carriage, resonating with a heady sense of possibility.

Marianne, ever the observant maid, shifted uncomfortably on the plush seat opposite Lady Emily. She had spent the past five years watching the captivating charm of her mistress blossom, often spurred on by the ebb and flow of her lively friends. Yet, buried beneath that effervescent exterior, Marianne was keenly aware of the insecurities that flickered like a candle in a draught. Lady Emily yearned for validation, often gauging her worth through the fleeting attentions of suitors and the laughter of her acquaintances. It struck Marianne as inherently unfair that Lady Emily's happiness was often tethered to the winds of societal whims. Although she treasured Lady Emily's spirited nature, she felt an overwhelming impulse to protect her from the absurdity of her latest scheme.

"Lady Emily, I must speak plainly," Marianne began, her voice steady yet laced with concern. "Lord Grey is a notorious rake, renowned for his reckless pursuits. You cannot simply ignore that. This bet you've made... it could lead to chaos." She watched as Lady Emily's eyes sparkled with enthusiasm, the truth in her words threatened to be cast aside. "The last thing you need is to entangle yourself with a man like him, who relishes in scandal. You deserve better than a passing whim inspired by some mischievous dare. Think wisely, my lady." Marianne could almost hear the steady cadence of her own heartbeat as she tried to convey her worries while the lanterns outside blurred into a flow of light, mirroring the dichotomy of excitement and dread within her.

Lady Emily ignored her. "It was as if he was telling me I could do anything! Can you imagine? What if we actually elope? It would be glorious—utterly scandalous!"

Marianne, whose expression had remained a thin veneer of amusement, watched with a kind of trepidation. She admired Lady Emily's spirit but felt the weight of reality pressing upon her, a growing concern etched on her brow.

"Your Ladyship," she began, choosing her words carefully, "while the night was indisputably delightful, one must consider the implications of such—*daring* decisions."

"Implications? Nonsense!" Emily interjected, her eyes bright with fervor. "This is our chance, Marianne! To reclaim adventure laden with the scent of roses and forbidden romance. Nothing more vivifying than a moonlit escape!"

Marianne sighed inwardly, struck by the juxtaposition of Lady Emily's excitement and her own reluctance. Yet deep within her heart, she couldn't help but be swept up in Lady Emily's enthusiasm, even as a voice of caution echoed quietly in her mind.

As the carriage rolled to a stop, Lady Emily's eyes sparkled with determination. "We must act, Marianne. We cannot let this opportunity slip away!"

"Are you truly suggesting you elope tonight?" Marianne gasped, unsure if she should laugh or scoff at the very idea. "Think of the chaos that could ensue! Your family!"

"Nonsense," Lady Emily declared, her voice rising slightly, mingling with the cool night air. "They wouldn't understand, but you do! Join me, leave the confines of decorum!"

Marianne opened her mouth, trying to reason with Lady Emily's enthusiasm, but words dissolved into a mixture of disbelief and acceptance. Lady Emily, now fully caught up in her own fervor, waved her hands animatedly, concocting ideas as the dream of rebellion swelled within her.

"We shall create a plan. A covert mission. Perhaps to the secluded garden by the river where I shall meet him," she exclaimed, eyes alight with mischief.

They both tumbled from the carriage, rushing into the safety of the manor, a sense of adventure washing over them. Lady Emily bounded into her room, the walls shrouded in the stillness of night, and Marianne hesitated at the door.

As Lady Emily flung herself onto her opulent bed, the soft rustling of silks and satins echoed in the quiet room. The moonlight poured through the window, casting a silvery glow across the elegant décor, yet the serene atmosphere did not match the tempest brewing within Marianne's heart.

"Lady Emily, you must listen to reason," Marianne urged, stepping quietly into the room, her expression a mixture of concern and exasperation. She busied herself with closing the heavy curtains before turning back to her mistress, her hands nervously smoothing any imagined wrinkles in her gown.

"Mari, you simply do not grasp the magnificence of it all!" Emily exclaimed, a bright smile illuminating her face in defiance of the constraints that bound women's hearts. "Imagine the exhilaration of storming into the unknown!"

Marianne cast a sideways glance at her mistress, who now toyed with the delicate lace of her nightgown. "Excitement is one thing. Recklessness is quite another."

Emily waved her off, her cheeks still flushed from the excitement of the night. "But isn't that what life is meant to be? Full of surprises?"

"Surprises, yes. Scandals, no," Marianne countered firmly, the weight of countless warnings and whispered stories trembling on her lips. "You may not know all there is to Lord Grey. The whispers, the tales... they are everywhere. He has left a trail of broken hearts and scandal in his wake."

Emily rolled her eyes, a gesture familiar to the ladies throughout high society, yet it stung with an edge of unwillingness. "I prefer not to indulge in such rumors, my dear Connelly. Unless one has evidence, the tales are naught but envy disguised as caution."

"Very well, but you cannot ignore the truth of his reputation," Marianne began, her insistence deepening as she approached Lady Emily, placing a comforting hand on her shoulder. "They say he leads young ladies to ruin—abandonment and sorrow left in his wake. That he is a scoundrel who seeks only frivolous delights. These are facts, not merely gossip."

"In any love story, is there not an element of risk? Emotions run high, and that is the beauty of it!" Emily said, her resolve thrumming with passion. "What I intend is to marry him, and I shall do so regardless of the whispers. I refuse to bound myself by the constraints that govern our lives."

Marianne sighed deeply, a slight frown creasing her brow. "But think of your family's reputation, Lady Emily! You are the daughter of a Viscount; your future cannot be leading the very man who flouts societal standards!"

Lady Emily shrugged, a wistful smile threatening to betray her earnestness. "Perhaps it is time to redefine those standards. When have I ever fit neatly into the mold? I am tired of pretending to be a dutiful daughter when inside I yearn for adventure."

"Adventure is not worth your dignity," Marianne replied, frustration rising. "And while I support your dreams, to nod and agree with such a reckless wager... I can hardly bear it." She turned away, pacing the room, feeling the urge to abandon the whole conversation rather than watch Lady Emily chase fantasies that could lead to heartbreak.

"When I dream of Lord Grey, I see more than the reputation of a rake," Emily said softly, almost to herself, a dreamy expression appearing in her eyes. "His charm is intoxicating. I wish for passion, Marianne! Can there be harm in wanting more than what is expected?"

"Passion can be a trap," Marianne countered, again fighting back against the urgency threatening to tip Lady Emily into the depths of folly. "I cannot bear to see you hurt—not by him, or anyone else for that matter. These whims of spontaneity may lead you somewhere you're not prepared to go."

With an exasperated swing of her arms, Lady Emily shook her head, her voice stronger now. "But what if he is different? What if he desires more than shallow flirtations? What if I *am* his match? I am not a child to cower in fear of shadows suggested by the whisperings of jealous tongues."

"I only wish for you to be happy," Marianne said, her heart heavy as she stepped closer and faced her dearest friend.

"I *will* be happy, and I'll find it with the Earl—scandalous as it may be," Emily insisted, unyielding. "Even if it means enduring the sharpest barbs of gossip."

"Where is your sense? This scheme spawned from a careless dare! I fear your heart will come to regret the price of such a choice," Marianne lamented dramatically, casting a glance at the finely embroidered tapestry that adorned the walls.

"True love may well come at a price, dear Marianne," Emily replied, a gentle defiance illuminating her expression. "Not every lady's tale must lead to a loveless betrothal. There exists a singular path for each of us beyond mere expectations."

Marianne stepped back, mulling over the intensity of her mistress's words. Though she relished the fiery spirit of Lady

Emily, concern gripped her all the tighter now. Emotion, especially in such a captivating yet treacherous venture, could lead to disastrous ends.

"Why must you curse this endeavor? Life is short. I refuse to squander my youth playing the obsequious daughter," Emily declared with newfound fervor.

The room fell into an uneasy silence, with Lady Emily beginning to shift into her nightgown—a soft blush gown trimmed with delicate lace. Summoning every ounce of restraint, Marianne could not abide the ensuing connection between them being tainted by ignorance.

"Lady Emily, I simply cannot advocate for this reckless pursuit any longer," she finally stated, her voice finding a firmer footing amidst the swirling chaos. The finality of her tone drew Lady Emily's attention, yet the warmth she had always known solidified suddenly into a colder light.

"What do you imply, Marianne?" Emily's brows furrowed, tension stringing the words like fine silk. "Will you abandon me in this quest?"

"I will not witness you soar toward danger, blindfolded," Marianne replied, voice taut. For a moment, she hesitated, measuring the weight of her words. "I shall not be a part of this foolish bet, my lady. When the sun rises, I can only hope that you think wisely before embracing what awaits you."

With that, she moved to the door, the closing sound echoing in the silence but harder still than the heart of the matter. Emily watched her leave, the tension settling uncomfortably between them, each moment of silence punctuated by uncertainty.

And as Marianne disappeared down the corridor, Lady Emily felt a flicker of doubt beneath all the bravado, crumbling under the weight of solitude. The room felt suddenly smaller, shadows creeping into the corners where their spirited plans had once danced in the light of moonbeams.

CHAPTER FOUR
morning calm
EDWARD, THE EARL OF GREY

Morning sunlight streamed through the sheer curtains of Lord Grey's lavish bedroom, casting an ethereal glow across the finely appointed furnishings that spoke of nobility and sophistication. The remnants of the previous night's soirée lingered faintly—echoing laughter and flirtatious banter faded into the calm of the morning.

Edward stirred awake, the world outside his window blissfully unaware of the scandal that had played out mere hours before. The chaotic energy of the ball had given way to tranquility that beckoned him to linger in the comfort of his sheets. However, the serenity was abruptly interrupted by the soft rap of knuckles against his door.

"Your lordship, may I enter?"

The voice of his dedicated servant, Thomas, disrupted the stillness, and Edward groaned softly as he propped himself up on one elbow, tousled dark hair falling charmingly into his eyes.

"Enter," he commanded, stretching as the door opened.

Thomas sauntered in, a knowing expression etched onto his face as he presented a small envelope on a silver tray. The delicate seal, unmistakably '**P**' for '**Percy**', piqued Edward's interest.

"From Lady Emily Percy, my lord. I thought you might wish to… examine it at your leisure," Thomas remarked, his tone indicating the delicate nature of the correspondence.

Edward took the envelope, feeling its weight. Lady Emily's careful script danced enticingly on the front, calling to him with every swirl and flourish. He slid it open, the anticipation tickling the back of his mind, and began to read.

As he scanned the contents, his eyebrows lifted in surprise. There was an unmistakable thrill in her words, an invitation to meet him beneath the veil of night. Her tone brimmed with adventure—an exhilarating blend of flirtation and daring; she had a tendre for a rebellion that mirrored his own.

I am weary of the constraints placed upon me by society...

the letter read, and a smirk creased Edward's lips at her audacity. He admired Lady Emily's spirit, recalling the sparkle in her expressive blue eyes, the way her laughter rang like a bell amid the stiff decorum of the ton. A far-off memory of her radiance danced in his mind.

He paused, a swirl of intrigue and unease settling in the pit of his stomach. This was a risk—emotional and social. He had never aimed to become entangled with a lady of her station, yet her words dug at the corners of his heart, urging him toward the very reckless abandon he typically embraced.

Reading further, he felt the familiar pull of both temptation and regret gnawing at him. *How easily she could be seduced!* Her eagerness to indulge in what lay outside the gilded cage of their society fanned the flames of his desire, igniting an excitement that threatened to consume him.

What would her family think? What would the ton say? But as his imagination hovered over visions of their escapade, filled with whispers and stolen glances under the cover of night, he found himself dismissing the usual hesitations that often held him captive. Perhaps Lady Emily sought revolution, but secretly, so did he.

And then, in a moment of clarity, he realized his decision was already forming. The allure of night had become irresistible. He envisioned her: hair catching the silvery glow of the moon, laughter mingling with the turning of the cool night air, exulting in their shared mischief as they danced at the edge of propriety. Her nakedness, with him rooted within.

So, pulling a quill and fresh parchment from his desk, his heart raced. He began writing down every detail that would guide their adventure—every planned route, every diversion. The meeting would transpire flawlessly, and they would escape into the wild tapestry of London's streets, hidden among the shadows of the city that looked down on their antics with both scorn and envy.

He recalled the secret inn tucked away, far from prying eyes, where he had tasted freedom before. A place often shrouded in rumors of clandestine gatherings and whispered seductions. It beckoned him like a siren, promising privacy away from the suffocating expectations of the aristocracy.

Painting a mental picture of how the night would unfold, his plans unfurled like a bright banner. He could arrive unnoticed, created distractions if need be, and whisk her away from the very confines that sought to restrain them both. The thrill of the chase ignited a flame within him, each breath he took filled with the intoxicating promise of their shared recklessness.

He paused, a sly grin forming at the thought of the shallow morals he'd toy with—the notion that he could ruin her with his allure yet walk away unscathed. The temptation thrilled him, not as cruelty but as an enticing avenue toward freedom. But deep within the recesses of his guilt-ridden conscience, there flickered a resistance to such selfishness.

"Tonight will be different," he muttered to himself, straightening as he contemplated what Lady Emily would wear, how they would sweep through London—the thrill of each stolen moment.

Edward slipped into a meticulously tailored coat, smoothing the fabric over his athletic frame. Each movement felt deliberate, every detail thus far serving to enhance the rogue he had cultivated. He caught his reflection in the mirror; a dashing distortion of society itself, daring and beguiling.

With a final glance in the looking glass, he combed back his hair, the thrill of the adventure taut in his chest. The night's possibilities unfurled before him, a canvas unmarked—just waiting for the brush of their escapade.

Stepping outside, the cool night air washed over him, awakening all his senses. He inhaled deeply, the faint scents of coal smoke and flowers mingling in both a reminder of home and a call to the unknown.

As he began to make his way down the cobbled streets, each echo of his steps sent surges through him. The world felt at once electrified with potential and shrouded in shadows where forbidden encounters could thrive. Dreams of daring deeds danced like fireflies at dusk.

A sudden rush of exhilaration washed over him—an intoxicating mixture of desire and ruin. Lady Emily, a spirited woman who had convincingly broken free from the chain of society, embodied the thrill of the night and the essence of adventure he craved. Together, they would craft an undisclosed tale against the backdrop of London's sleeping streets.

Tonight could change everything.

CHAPTER FIVE
a london garden

The sun dipped below the horizon, casting a soft twilight over London. In her elegantly adorned bedroom, Lady Emily's heart raced with exhilaration, the thrill of her decision surging through her like the rush of a summer storm. The soft rustle of her letter, now crinkled in her hand, ignited her spirit—she had taken the audacious step of inviting Lord Grey to meet her in a secluded garden later that night.

"Marianne!" Emily's voice, filled with giddy anticipation, broke through the stillness. The sound of cascading laughter echoed faintly from outside, but inside their domestic bubble, all that existed was the electrifying secret she was bursting to share.

Marianne, emerged from the door, her chestnut hair gleaming with the dim light from the chandelier. "What is it, my lady?" She spoke with a quirked eyebrow, sensing the electric charge in the air.

"I've sent him a letter!" Emily exclaimed, her blue eyes alight with mischief. "He replied almost immediately, suggesting we meet at the gardens tonight."

A deep frown creased Marianne's brow, her heart plummeting with the realization of what this entailed. "You cannot be serious, Lady Emily. This is madness. We are not eloping to become the scandal of the season on a mere whim."

"Madness or not, it's adventure!" Emily's reply came skipping through the air like a lighthearted melody. She twirled on her heels, earning a sulky look from Marianne, before continuing. "Marianne, you've always said I should break free of this monotonous existence! Now is my chance! Just imagine—an evening filled with excitement!"

"Excitement that could end in disaster!" Marianne protested, folding her arms across her chest. "There are so many complications that could arise. What if anyone sees us? What if Lord Grey has other intentions?"

Ignoring her ladymaid's concerns, Lady Emily's enthusiasm became infectious. "Perhaps it is precisely his intentions I desire," she breathed, her cheeks blooming with color. "Now, help me prepare!"

With a resigned sigh mingled with fond exasperation, Marianne conceded. "Very well, but we must move quickly and discreetly. Your reputation will undoubtedly suffer if we are discovered."

With a shared understanding, the atmosphere shifted, anticipation wrapping around them as they rummaged through Emily's carefully crafted wardrobe, their giggles echoing softly against the walls. Unusual for the confines of their elegant lives, they finally slipped into darker clothing—practical yet hinting at hidden elegance, with Emily joining in on the frivolity of disguising their refined social identities.

"I believe this cloak will suit you beautifully, my lady," Marianne teased as she draped a dark fabric over Lady Emily's shoulders, the garment contrasting sharply against the soft pastels of her usual attire. The sight caused a burst of laughter to erupt between them, the ridiculousness of the situation whirling around them like a waltz.

"You wear a cloak too, Marianne. I cannot have anyone recognizing you either," Lady Emily remarked, her voice laced with playful urgency as she rounded up her things. The soft rustle of fabric accompanied her movements, a testament to her excitement and determination to blend into the shadows of the evening.

With their plan solidifying, they donned their new attire, adjusting capes here, lacing corsets there. All the while, they quietly reveled in the thought of adventure that lay ahead.

Finally, a nervous thrill transformed into sheer excitement as they prepared to sneak out. Heartbeats echoed in their ears, and whispers filled the air, heavy with delight and trepidation.

"Remember, we must tread softly," Marianne instructed, leading the way down the candlelit corridor.

The silence of the house enveloped them, every creak of the floor amplifying their furtive movements. As they reached the door, Marianne glanced over her shoulder with wide eyes.

Suddenly, in the midst of her caution, she stumbled over the hem of her gown. The collision sent her toppling forward, and Emily barely managed to stifle a giggle as she caught her friend by the elbow, holding her steady.

"Perhaps we should have chosen something a touch shorter," Lady Emily chuckled, her laughter dancing through the stillness as they repositioned themselves.

"That would have been wise, wouldn't it?" Marianne replied, her voice low, punctuated with laughter that threatened to spill into the darkened halls. Finally stabilizing herself, she composure returned. "Now, onward!"

They eased the door open, revealing the moonlit street outside. The vibrancy of London at night spread out before them. Gaslights flickered, casting a golden glow on cobblestone streets bustling with carriages painted against the night and the distant sound of music wafting through the air from nearby soirées.

"Look how lively the city appears under the moonlight," Emily remarked as they stepped into the cool night air, her voice barely above a whisper.

"Lively, indeed," Marianne replied, caution enveloping her words. "But it is not just passersby and carriages that are to be concerned about."

With excitement thrumming at her heart, Lady Emily brushed aside her friend's protests. "Do not fret. Here lies our grand adventure."

As they made their way through the winding roads, anticipation mounted. The world around them faded, leaving only thoughts of the delightful rendezvous that awaited. Flowers perfumed the night air as they approached a secluded garden, the entrance obscured by gracefully overhanging vines.

Upon entering, the vibrant blooms illuminated against the night's shadowy tapestry filled Emily's senses. The air was sweetened with the fragrance of roses, petals reflecting the dim light as if the garden were sprinkled with stars. "It truly is beautiful," she whispered.

"Indeed," Marianne responded, but her eyes darted anxiously, scanning the edges of the garden as if to reassure herself that their scheme would not collapse.

They found a quaint spot beneath a venerable old oak, and it was there that their delightful banter resumed, bubbling over with nervous energy.

"What do you think Lord Grey will say?" Emily asked, a dreamy smile gracing her lips. "Will he be surprised? Or, perhaps, he will be amused at my daring nature?"

"Amused? I'd venture to say he may be astonished," Marianne replied dryly, not entirely convinced of the venue's romantic merit, her tone light but hinting at her apprehension. "Lord Grey isn't known for being reputable about adventure, remember?"

"True, but this adventure is one of my own making!" Emily declared resolutely, her eyes sparkling with hope. "Just consider —who could have foreseen this? I shall be not merely another face at society's soirées!"

As they continued to chatter, laughter mingling with the night air, Marianne couldn't help but feel the enchantment of the moment, even as shadows of doubt lingered just beneath the surface. She cast her mind back to past ventures undone by whimsical fancy and candid desires.

Yet, as their conversation flowed, a sudden hush fell over them; the unmistakable sound of approaching footsteps reverberated in the stillness. Emily's excitement surged, but Marianne felt a coil of concern tighten in her throat once more.

"Perhaps we should reconsider," she suggested, casting anxious glances toward where the footsteps grew louder. Lady Emily, however, merely shook her head, mischief dancing on her features.

CHAPTER SIX
mistaken intentions

The night air hung thick with excitement as Lady Emily and her lady's maid, Miss Connelly, huddled beneath the sheltering branches of a sprawling oak in the secluded garden. Moonlight filtered through the leaves, casting dappled shadows that danced across the ground, and the heady scent of blooming jasmine enveloped them like a comforting blanket. The garden, filled with silver flowers and swaying leaves, held the promise of an enjoyable evening.

Upon the darkened path, Lady Emily adjusted her cloak, its fabric whispering against her skin. The midnight blue material concealed her elegant gown, yet somehow felt liberating in its practicality. "Marianne, do stop worrying. I assure you, it's simply a moonlit stroll. What could possibly go awry?" Her laughter bubbled from her lips, light as the gentle breeze that played around them.

Marianne clasped her hands tightly against her chest, her heart pounding in rhythm with the unease that flooded her veins. "A moonlit stroll, my lady, on the very night you've dared to elope with a rake? You may wish to rethink your definition of simple."

She frowned, glancing nervously about as if the very shadows might harbor some omniscient being to condemn them.

"You have far too vivid an imagination," Emily teased, her blue eyes sparkling with mischief under the moon's pale glow. "Perhaps it's the scent of the jasmine intoxicating you."

Marianne inhaled sharply, appreciating the heady fragrance that intensified with each soft rustle of the leaves. Yet, for all its sweetness, it brought with it an undercurrent of doubt that twisted uneasily in her stomach. "This does not feel like a fairytale, Lady Emily. Recklessness and romantic dreams rarely yield pleasant results."

The tension escalated. Still, there was a certain thrill in their seclusion, an allure to the dangers of their escapade. Lady Emily leaned against the rough bark of the oak, her heart hammering in anticipation of Lord Edward Grey's arrival. "Oh, do not be such a prude, Marianne! Have we not been deprived of excitement long enough? Tonight, we reclaim a bit of adventure." She flicked her hair back, the golden curls shimmering in the moonlight.

The darkness swelled around Lady Emily and Marianne, thickening like a heavy curtain, yet sprinkled with the soft glow of gas lamps that lined the distant streets. Flickering flames illuminated the cobblestones, casting elongated shadows and shaping the night into a chiaroscuro of light and dark. The air turned cool and fragrant, infused with the delicate perfume of roses that wove through the garden, mingling serenely with the scent of damp earth.

Emily's heart raced as she squinted into the night, and her eagerness heightened when she spotted a figure emerging from the depths of the shadows. "Marianne, look!" Her whispers carried the thrill of anticipation. "Could it be him?"

Marianne shifted, her gaze fixated on the silhouette now moving closer. For a fleeting moment, doubt pricked at her, casting a veil of uncertainty. "I can't tell," she murmured, a frown creasing her brow as she teetered between hope and caution. "It could simply be someone returning home after a night of revelry. Shall we hide further among the flowers?"

"No, I must see!" Lady Emily's spirited nature ignited a spark that could not be contained. She stepped forward, her insistence brushing aside any moments of prudence. "If that is Lord Grey, I shall not let the opportunity slip through my fingers."

Hushed between the whispers of the leaves, the sounds of night embraced them—a faint rustle of the garden's flora, the distant chuckle of waters from a nearby stream, and the echo of laughter that floated from the grand soirées taking place beyond the garden walls. As the figure drew nearer, the moon unveiled itself from behind a cloud, bathing the garden in a silvery luminosity, and illuminating the curious eyes of Lady Emily. With bated breath, she clutched the fabric of her cloak and edged into the light.

Marianne's heart raced as she witnessed Lady Emily dart toward the man walking toward them; an irresistible force with the gravity of mischief pulling her along. It was a tableau of two worlds colliding, and the lady's maid felt the urgent need to intervene, torn between loyalty and rising alarm.

Marianne decided to sprint alongside her. "Lady Emily!" she hissed, her voice laden with apprehension as she reached out to grasp the fabric of Lady Emily's cloak. "Do not take another step! You do not know what game you are playing."

But Lady Emily, lost in sensual excitement, shrugged off Marianne's hand as she made her approach toward the dashing rake. "What game?" she quipped, casting a glance over her shoulder, her blue eyes shimmering with defiance. "This is precisely where I wish to be, Marianne—there is no game at play as far as I can see."

That notion was perilously false, and Marianne's throat constricted as the very core of her friend's ill-timed boldness laid bare before her. "You cannot—" she began, but the words caught in a flutter of concern, replaced by a sharp gasp as Lady Emily stumbled on the uneven cobblestones.

"Watch—" Emily cried, her laughter abruptly wafting into a shocked silence before she regained her balance and fixed Marianne with a sharp glare. "You must cease this incessant worry, Marianne! You act as if I need your protection."

"I do not think it is protection you require, my lady," came Marianne's retort, the exasperation mixing with a hint of humiliation. As her pulse surged through her veins, she wrestled with the embarrassment of clumsiness echoing through the night. "What favor could possibly redeem you in the eyes of Lord Grey if you tip so carelessly before him?"

The moment froze as Emily's bright cheeks turned an even deeper shade of pink under the moonlight, and the reproach hung between them thick as fog. "He cannot discern my worth based on a stumble, surely!" Lady Emily declared, more indignation simmering in her tone than she had intended.

"You misunderstand me," Marianne pressed, her brows knitting together as she spoke softly into the tense atmosphere. "It is the principle of the matter. This reckless pursuit may have consequences far wider than your delicate ambition."

"Consequences," scoffed Lady Emily, brushing off the gravity of it all with a flick of her wrist, forcing down the swell of annoyance rising within her. "Perhaps your dearest dreams have led you to forget your station, Marianne. You are a *lady's maid*, and it is wise you remember your place. You are simply here to assist *me*."

The words struck Marianne like a sharp blade, slicing through the humor and light of the moment, leaving only bitterness. She bit her lip, attempting to swallow the urge to flinch. "And you are the daughter of a Viscount," she replied, trying to keep her voice steady, but the effort only highlighted the betrayal that stung from Emily's harsh reminder. "A confounding reality I shall never forget, my lady."

With a scowl crinkling her brow, Lady Emily took a measured breath, the passion countered by the realization that Marianne's loyalty in this moment could not be taken lightly. Yet, the indignation still fluttered at the edges of her heart as if daring her to act foolishly. "I do not require your reminders to know who I am. I seek adventure, not the dull expectations you seem so keen on enforcing. Lord Grey is here now, and that is the only truth that matters!"

Before she could utter another word, Lady Emily turned away from Marianne, striding purposefully to the alluring figure of Lord Grey. The gaiety swirling in her chest drowned out the fleeing doubt as he drew closer, but Marianne, heart heavy, refused to let go of her watchful role. She knew all too well that this game was not simply an innocent whim; the stakes stood higher than any of them could dare perceive.

"Lady Emily," she hissed in the darkness, imploringly, enduring the disapproving gaze of society even as they flitted about their nightly gatherings. "This is a dangerous dance—"

But the words fell like rain upon thorns, for Lady Emily merely waved her hand dismissively over her shoulder, clearly enamored by whatever charms Lord Edward could offer. With his roguish appeal and undeniable air of excitement, it was all she could do not to melt into his presence.

Disappointed, Marianne watched Lady Emily dissolve into the darkness. Accepting her fate, playing with fire.

THE MOON HUNG high in the London sky, a watchful sentinel over the city's quiet hours. Lord Edward Grey slipped through the shadows of the garden, drawn onwards with a heady mix of excitement and anticipation. The scents of blooming jasmine and night-blooming flowers enveloped him, enhancing the intoxicating aura of the nighttime rendezvous. He had considered the evening an opportunity for mischief, a chance to whisk away Lady Emily Percy into a world of adventure that transcended their gilded cages.

Yet, as he moved stealthily, weaving through the arbors and pathways, a flicker of something else danced in his chest—an inkling that perhaps this escapade was about to be something unlike any other.

Stepping closer, his hopeful gaze searched for the familiar figure he yearned to meet, the one who had awakened long-buried feelings within him. Just then, an idea seized him, an impulse straight from the whimsical pages of romantic tales he often scoffed at. With a mischievous grin, he tugged his heavy cloak tighter about him—it seemed the very perfect prop for the evening's planned theatrics. The intent was to drape it over Lady Emily, enveloping her in its warmth and shadow, imparting an air of mystery to their elopement.

Then he saw her.

Her slender frame within a cloak of mystery.

With his heart drumming a thrilling tempo, he sneaked towards the spot where he believed she awaited him. Shadows flickered as he moved, the moonlight casting playful patterns on the ground.

Then, in a moment of exuberance, he swooped down, throwing the cloak over a squirming figure that gasped beneath its heavy folds.

"Heavens, my lady! How delightful to take you by surprise!" he called, laughter escaping his lips as he hoisted the figure over his shoulder without a second thought. His mind whirled at the prospect of their escape, the thrill of indulging in a reckless, unpredictable adventure intoxicating him further with each step he took.

With a playful bounce, he began striding towards the carriage waiting just beyond the garden's edge, oblivious to the confusion stirring beneath the cloak. Instead of her laughter ringing in his ears, he heard muffled protests; the figure wriggled against his shoulders.

"Fear not, dear Emily, I shall whisk you away to greener pastures." He chuckled and stole a glance beneath the cloak, his heart swelling with exhilaration at how fate seemed to conspire in his favor, bringing him the most intoxicating woman in all of London.

"Just think of all the scandalous adventures that await us," he continued, lost in the enthusiasm of recounting tales of escapades —exploits that danced dangerously close to the edge of propriety. "Why, just last week, I narrowly escaped a mad bull at Lord Stanhope's estate! They say it was the hottest topic of the week, but you, Emily—you shall add your own chapter to my realm of daring stunts."

Beneath the heavy cloak, the figure squirmed again, this time more vehemently. Edward paid no mind, still wrapped in the daydream of heroics and romance. His thoughts danced around how enticing it would be for Emily to hear that he had already made arrangements at a discreet inn, far removed from the prying eyes of Society—the perfect spot for their elopement and an adventure that promised excitement at every turn.

As they moved forward, entering the shadowed outskirts of the garden, Edward kept on with his charming anecdotes. "Ah, did I ever share the tale of how I outwitted the Duchess of Beddlington in a game of charades? It is a marvel, really, how easily one can cast aside the expectations of the ton with merely a wink and a laugh!"

Just as they reached the carriage, Edward hoisted the cloak-covered figure and intending to place her gently inside, took hold of her waist, the gesture meant to elicit a sense of grand romance. With a flourish that only a man steeped in high society could manage, he tossed his burden into the carriage. "Off we go, then! Post haste!" he called out to his footman, who was already situated at the front, barely concealing his astonishment.

"Your Grace?" the footman replied, eyes wide as he looked back. Edward waved a hand, hardly noticing the cocked brow.

"Leave this cursed place! We are bound for more intriguing horizons!"

As the carriage jolted to life, Edward settled down beside her, the heat of his anticipation enveloping them both. He turned to the cloaked figure next to him, eager to gauge her delight, but was met with the muffled sounds of protest.

"It seems my lady has quite a penchant for mischief herself," he grinned, brushing aside the mild confusion that started to stir. *What was a cloak without its share of playful antics?*

"Ah, what fun this shall be!" he exclaimed, utterly engrossed in his recounting of a firework-laden escapade he'd had the previous summer, a caper that seemed a mere whisper of memory now, so far removed from the rush of emotions that coursed through him at present.

Yet the figure beside him remained silent, and the weight of her sudden stillness intrigued him. His brow furrowed slightly as he shifted to catch a better glimpse of her through the dim light.

CHAPTER SEVEN
the abduction

The carriage rattled along the cobblestone road, the light from a lantern flickering intermittently as if caught in a playful dance with the darkness outside. Marianne found herself still in a bemused daze from the unexpected turn of events. One moment, she was preparing for a covert rendezvous between her friend and the notorious Lord Edward Grey, and the next *she* was ensconced against the plush upholstery of a lavish carriage, a heavy cloak enveloping her like a cocoon. *At least she saved Lady Emily from certain ruin.*

As adrenaline coursed through her, she took a deep breath, collecting her wits. Edward sat opposite her, looking entirely too pleased with himself. The thrill of adventure was palpable, but restrained laughter bubbled beneath the surface as she prepared to engage in verbal fencing.

With the hood of her cloak still covering her eyes, she quipped, "Well, I must commend you, my lord, for an entrance befitting a grand romantic novel—but do tell, is this how you treat all your notable trysts? Slung haphazardly over your shoulder like a bag of potatoes?"

Edward chuckled, clearly missing the deeper implications of her sarcasm. "I do have a penchant for grand gestures. You must admit, it creates a certain sense of excitement." His eyes sparkled with mischief.

"Excitement, you say?" Marianne leaned in, sporting a charming smile. "A bit of warning might enhance the thrill, perhaps with actual consent? Imagine the headline:

'Notorious Rake Kidnaps Lady of Repute.'"

More laughter bubbled forth from Edward, though the confusion of the situation slowly began to penetrate the joyous facade he wore.

Marianne reveled in the need to keep him oblivious, an amusing game she could play, to dodge his probing questions about her identity without arousing suspicion. "What happens now?"

"What do you want to happen?" he mused, regarding her with a roguish grin.

"Perhaps I will take your lead," she suggested, her tone playful as the carriage slowed to a stop, causing her heart to flutter with anticipation.

They reached their destination, only to discover Edward in a decidedly unromantic state of mind. With a quick movement, he hauled her out of the carriage, effortlessly slinging her over his shoulder again. "Time to astound the crowd with our spectacular arrival—I'm a regular at this esteemed venue, so fear not, my darling, for we're practically invisible." He marched toward the inn's entrance, his enthusiasm seemingly unaffected by the tempest brewing within.

Marianne nearly protested but was cut short by the rush of the night air wrapping around them, carrying a medley of distant voices and laughter. As Edward pushed through the doors of the tavern, the warm glow of firelight spilled onto their faces, illuminating the chattering throng.

The atmosphere was alive with the raucous sounds of laughter and the buzzing chatter of patrons, their curious eyes shifting toward the surprising pair as they entered. Questions darted through the air like pesky bugs, eager to land on the latest scandal.

"Another one, Lord Grey?" a voice called out, laced with teasing incredulity.

"Third one this month!" another patron chimed in, igniting a fresh wave of laughter that rippled through the crowd.

Edward, unfazed and ever the charming rogue, smiled at their playful jabs, his green eyes glinting with mischief. With a flourish, he deposited the woman from his shoulder, the cloak that had shrouded her falling away to reveal not the anticipated figure of Lady Emily, but rather the captivating visage of a mysterious unknown woman. A hush fell over the crowd as they leaned in, intrigued by this unexpected twist in the evening's entertainment.

*Who was **she**?*

Clad in the modest attire of a servant, the crisp white apron draped over her dress served as an unmistakable marker of her station. Yet, the simplicity of her garments could not conceal the striking beauty that radiated from her. With features that could easily be mistaken for those of a lady of higher standing, she was undeniably captivating—an unexpected and delightful mistake.

His expression morphed from devil-may-care confidence to stunned disbelief, mouth parting in surprise. "You," he began, trailing off in confusion, his mind racing to comprehend the tangled web he had spun. "...are *not* Lady Percy ... who the hell are you?"

"Miss Connelly, at your service," she curtsied, a playful grin on her lips as the tavern erupted with catcalls and whistles, the patrons reveling in the unexpected drama unfolding before them. "It appears you've mistaken me for a lady of far greater stature."

The atmosphere shifted as Edward's frantic internal dialogue spiraled. "What madness is this?" he murmured under his breath, grappling with the absurdity of his actions as the air thickened with gossiping energy. "I've abducted the maid..."

The onlookers burst into laughter, their amusement echoing through the tavern as they clicked their glasses together, celebrating the chaotic scene that had just unfolded from their lost and won wagers.

Edward, however, was far from amused. His expression darkened with irritation as he swiftly reached for Marianne's arm, yanking her away from the raucous crowd and dragging her toward a quieter corner of the tavern, where the noise faded into a muffled hum. His heart raced, both from the thrill of the moment and the need to regain control over the spiraling absurdity that seemed to envelop them.

"Miss Connelly, you say?" He asked through gritted teeth.

"Yes, and you might want to reconsider your method of pursuit, my lord," Marianne replied, a mischievous glimmer in her hazel eyes. "If you wanted to sweep someone off their feet, a dark garden is hardly the stage upon which to perform such."

The unexpected jibe twisted inside Edward's mind, flickering remnants of interest gathering at the edge of his curiosity. "I suppose I expected more dainty decorum from Lady Percy."

He couldn't help but chuckle again; the absurdity of the situation struck him as laughingly ludicrous, yet the simmering frustration that lay just beneath the surface begged to break free. A part of him sought a clever retort to reclaim some semblance of control over their ludicrous predicament.

"You, dear, do not speak of one equal to your station," he breathed, his voice laced with irritation. Each word felt like an empty dagger that fell flat against the vivacity radiating from her hazel eyes. *How did a mere maid wield such boldness, daring to ensure his cavalier reputation bore the brunt of her words?*

Yet, as the moment hung suspended in the dim light of the tavern, Marianne's expression softened, and she drew a steady breath. "Perhaps it is not my station you should concern yourself with, my lord," she began, her voice calm but fiery beneath the surface. "It's more about what you seem willing to do to others—like Lady Emily."

Edward's amusement slipped, instantly replaced by a growing unease that had little to do with the trial of his reputation. "Lady Emily?" he echoed, puzzled. "What of her?"

"Her reputation and her choices are not playthings, you know," Marianne pressed on, her voice gaining strength as though she meant to gather momentum. "You may turn your reckless escapades into tales of gallantry, but the consequences are real. You toy with her whims and desires simply because it amuses you, do you not? Regardless of what you may think, she will not emerge unscathed should you continue this ridiculous charade."

The words struck Edward more deeply than he anticipated. At first, he remained at a total loss for words, his mind reeling from the collision of anger and intrigue that swirled within him. Here was a woman of lesser station, her impassioned plea blazing against the backdrop of his own careless existence. The louder her voice projected, the more drawn he became to her fiery spirit, which danced defiantly against the conventional image he had of those within her rank.

"You dare presume to lecture me on the repercussions of my actions?" Edward retorted, though the bite fell flat, undoubtedly failing to reach his intended target. The more she spoke, the more captivated he became by the passion in her voice, igniting that unnamable longing that the parties and flirtations of high society had failed to sate.

"Someone must," she countered, her brows knitted with determination. "If you cared even a fraction for Lady Emily beyond the thrill of your pursuit, you would consider the implications of such reckless behavior. You wish to indulge yourself in adventure without thought for the person you so carelessly whisk away to your own whims."

Her honesty held him still, unraveling the wall he typically put up to guard against emotions—uncomfortable yet fascinating emotions. Lord Edward found himself diving towards an unexpected tide, swept along by the newfound insight and perhaps a hint of vulnerability woven through her words, each syllable pricking at the conscience he had buried beneath layers of wit and charm.

"Do you think she is not aware of the path she chooses?" he demanded, feigning defiance while an internal battle raged on.

"I think she is caught in the dissipating glamour of the Season," Marianne replied, her tone laced with a sad, knowing clarity. "And blinded by mischief, much like you. But her heart is a fragile thing, my lord, and I'd wager that her dreams are not as delirious as yours. The question is whether you'll be the one who sees to it that they remain so."

The echoes of her sentiments lingered in the air, twisting around them amidst the low hum of tavern gossip and the clinking of tankards, igniting a disquieted fire deep within him—not quite pride, and certainly not the callousness he often wore like armor. He could simultaneously acquiesce to her astute observations while resolutely resisting the notion that her words held any weight. Yet here he was, feeling both intrigued and vexed as he absorbed her ardor underscored by the disappointment only someone of her innate vibrancy could convey.

Instead of summoning the arrogance he'd championed merely moments before, he found himself searching her face for clarity, rather than irritation, as she unknowingly tugged at the frayed edges of his carefully cultivated exterior. For the first time, he considered the perspective of someone who existed outside the gilded cage of high society, someone who transcended that world with unexpected complexity—her fiery gaze unwavering yet somehow empathetic.

"Perhaps the adventure you speak of may not be the one that unfolds tonight, but rather the turmoil of this reckless pursuit I grasp at," he murmured, that dangerous blend of attraction and vulnerability crackling in the air like lightning about to strike.

Edward's frustration deepened, but in some odd way, it intrigued him as well. A flicker of respect crept into his thoughts; this woman he had abducted was certainly not the meek sort he had initially assumed. "Very well, Miss Connelly," he conceded, fighting back the urge to chuckle at her audacity. "Let us see where this dance leads us."

The tension hung thick in the air, both of them caught in a game that entwined charm with chaos and unexpected attraction, leaving the tavern patrons in stitches while they both navigated their absurd situation.

In the flickering candlelight of the dimly lit corridor, Marianne's appearance took on an unexpected allure that captivated Edward's gaze. Her dark tresses, usually confined in a practical bun, had loosened during their escapade, allowing tendrils of silky strands to frame her delicate features. The simple muslin gown she wore as a lady's maid hugged her lithe form, accentuating the gentle curves that her modest attire often concealed.

A flush of excitement colored her cheeks, lending a rosy hue to her porcelain complexion, and her hazel eyes sparkled with a defiant spirit that seemed to challenge the very boundaries of her station. In that moment, Edward found himself entranced by the uncharted beauty that lay before him—a beauty that transcended the rigid confines of societal expectations and stirred something primal within him.

As he studied her, he couldn't help but wonder how he had failed to notice the alluring grace that now captivated him *so* completely. Marianne's unwavering gaze held his own, her lips curved into a tantalizing smile that hinted at secrets yet to be unveiled. Edward felt a sudden, inexplicable desire to unravel the mysteries that lay beneath her composed exterior, to explore the depths of her wit, her daring spirit, and what lay beneath her shift.

CHAPTER EIGHT
revelations on the road

"I've had enough of this charade," Edward quipped, his voice laced with playful defiance as he escorted Marianne through the bustling tavern, the lively atmosphere swirling around them.

Embarrassed, Marianne kept her head down, her cheeks flushed with a mix of mortification and excitement, as the patrons continued with their raucous catcalls, their laughter ringing in the air like a mischievous chorus celebrating their antics. Each jest and tease felt like a spotlight shining directly upon her, amplifying her desire to disappear into the wooden floorboards beneath her feet.

Once outside, the cool night air offered a reprieve from the stifling tavern. Edward ushered Marianne towards a waiting carriage, his heart pounding with a mix of exhilaration and trepidation. As he helped her inside, their fingers brushed ever so slightly, sending a jolt of electricity through his body.

The carriage interior was cloaked in shadows, the only illumination coming from the occasional flicker of a passing streetlamp. Marianne leaned back against the plush seat, her chest rising and falling as she caught her breath. A soft giggle escaped her lips, and Edward found himself chuckling in response, the absurdity of their situation not lost on either of them.

"Well, Miss Marianne," Edward began, his voice laced with amusement, "I must admit, this was not quite the adventure I had envisioned for the evening."

Marianne arched an eyebrow, her lips curling into a playful smirk. "Indeed, my lord. Though I must commend you on your daring attempt at romance."

Edward felt his cheeks flush, but he met her teasing gaze with a roguish grin. "Ah, but where would be the thrill in following convention? A true gentleman must always keep his lady guessing."

As the carriage lurched forward, the banter subsided, and a contemplative silence settled between them. Marianne's gaze drifted to the window, watching as the familiar streets of London rolled by. A twinge of uncertainty tugged at her heart as she pondered the implications of their impromptu escapade.

She had always prided herself on her practicality, her feet firmly planted on the ground even as Lady Emily's whimsical nature threatened to sweep her away. Yet, here she was, alone in a carriage with one of London's most notorious rakes, her reputation hanging perilously in the balance.

A part of her thrilled at the novelty of it all, the exhilarating rush of defying societal expectations. This was an adventure unlike any she had ever known, a night she would forever etch into her memory. But the rational voice in her head whispered of the consequences, the whispers and sideways glances that would inevitably follow.

Marianne stole a glance at Lord Edward, her breath catching in her throat as she took in his chiseled features, softened by the flickering candlelight. He was undeniably handsome, with an air of roguish charm that seemed to beckon her closer even as her better judgment warned her away.

With a soft sigh, she leaned back against the cushions, allowing herself to bask in the moment, to revel in the thrill of the unknown. For tonight, at least, she would cast aside her doubts and embrace the adventure that had so unexpectedly fallen into her lap.

THE CARRIAGE ROCKED GENTLY as it navigated the winding streets of London, the muffled sounds of the bustling city fading into the background. In the dimly lit interior, an air of uncertainty lingered between Edward and Marianne, the weight of their unexpected adventure settling upon them.

Edward broke the silence first, his voice tinged with a vulnerability that belied his usual rakish demeanor. "Apologies, Miss Connelly. You must think me a complete cad," he began, his green eyes searching Marianne's face. "Abducting a woman without a second thought, all in pursuit of some fleeting thrill." He paused, running a hand through his tousled hair as if gathering his thoughts. "The truth is, I've grown weary of the endless charades and shallow pursuits expected of a man of my station. There's a hollowness to it all, a constant yearning for something more substantial."

Marianne listened intently, her hazel eyes softening as Edward's words resonated within her. She recognized the weight of societal expectations, having navigated her own constraints as a lady's maid.

Edward's confession seemed to unlock a deeper understanding between them. "I know what it's like to feel trapped by the expectations placed upon you," Marianne replied, her voice gentle yet resolute. "To crave a life beyond the boundaries set by others."

Their gazes met, and in that moment, a silent acknowledgment passed between them – a recognition of kindred spirits yearning for something more profound than the roles society had assigned them.

Emboldened by their newfound connection, Marianne shared her own dreams of independence and adventure. "I've always longed for a life where I could forge my own path, free from the constraints of servitude," she confessed, her words carrying the weight of years of suppressed desires.

Edward listened intently, captivated by the strength and resilience that radiated from Marianne. He found himself drawn to her spirit, admiring the way she navigated the complexities of their situation with wit and grace.

As their conversation deepened, a playful tone emerged, and they began to speculate about the myths and tales associated with love and elopements. Marianne's eyes sparkled with mischief as she suggested increasingly outlandish scenarios, challenging Edward to entertain the notion of a lifelong partnership rooted in adventure.

Just as their banter reached its peak, the carriage jolted over a rough patch of road, causing them to tumble together in a tangle of laughter and limbs. In that moment, the weight of their circumstances seemed to dissipate, replaced by a shared sense of exhilaration and camaraderie.

As their laughter subsided, a charged silence fell over the carriage. Edward found himself captivated by the way the flickering lamplight danced across Marianne's features, accentuating the warmth in her eyes and the curve of her smile.

Without a word, they exchanged lingering glances, the air thick with an undeniable chemistry that neither could ignore. It was a pivotal moment, a shift in their dynamic that hinted at the possibility of something deeper blossoming between them.

Unable to resist the magnetic pull between them, Edward succumbed to the moment. With a gentle touch, he moved closer to Marianne, the warmth of her presence enveloping him. He cupped her face in his hands, the softness of her skin sending a jolt of electricity through his fingertips. As he gazed into her eyes, he found himself lost in their depths, the playful banter of moments ago giving way to a connection that transcended words.

Overwhelmed by an irresistible tenderness that belied his customary flirtatious nature, Edward inclined his head and seized Marianne's lips in a fervent embrace. The clamor of the world outside receded, abandoning them to the symphony of their pounding hearts and the intoxicating aroma of their mutual longing. The kiss was a revelation, a testament to the unvoiced connection that had emerged between them during their unforeseen escapade.

Edward's lips moved with deliberate slowness against Marianne's, savoring the sweetness of her mouth. He tasted the lingering remnants of the wine they had shared and felt a thrill of desire course through him. His fingers traced the delicate curve of her jaw, feeling the rapid flutter of her pulse beneath her skin.

Marianne responded with equal fervor, her hands slipping around his neck as she pulled him closer. She could feel the hard planes of his chest pressed against her, the heat of his body seeping through the thin fabric of her dress. Her nipples hardened in response, sending a jolt of pleasure straight to her core.

Edward's tongue flicked against her lips, seeking entrance, and Marianne opened to him without hesitation. Their tongues danced together, exploring and tasting each other with an intensity that left them both breathless. He could feel the softness of her breasts crushed against him, the hard peaks of her nipples pressing into his chest.

As the kiss deepened, Edward's hands roamed down Marianne's back, tracing the curve of her spine until they reached the swell of her hips. He pulled her tighter against him, grinding his hips into hers as he felt the unmistakable evidence of his arousal. Marianne moaned softly, her own desire building in response to his touch.

Edward wrenched himself away from Marianne's lips, panting heavily. His gaze fell to her chest, and with a swift motion, he pulled down the front of her bodice, revealing her breasts. He groaned at the sight of her hardened nipples, and his tongue darted out to taste them. He flicked and swirled his tongue around one nipple, then the other, relishing in the feel of her body responding to his touch. Marianne gasped, arching her back and pressing herself closer to him. Edward's hands roamed over her body, exploring every curve and contour with a hunger that left them both trembling. He could feel the heat radiating from her, and he knew that she was as desperate for him as he was for her.

Gently, he guided her towards the edge of the bench, their lips never breaking contact as they tumbled onto the soft surface. Edward's hands moved to Marianne's hips, pulling her on top of him as he positioned himself between her legs. He could feel the wetness of her desire, and he knew that they were both ready for what came next. With a slow, deliberate motion, he entered her, gasping at the sensation of her warmth enveloping him. They moved together in a rhythm that was as old as time itself, their bodies entwined as they climbed higher and higher. Edward could feel the tension building within him, and he knew that he was close to the edge. With one final, desperate thrust, he reached his climax, crying out Marianne's name as he spilled himself inside her. Marianne followed soon after, her body shaking with the force of her release. They sat there for a moment, panting and sweating, their bodies still connected as they slowly came back down to earth. Edward pulled Marianne close, holding her tightly as he knew life between them would never be the same.

As they pulled away, breathless and entwined, Edward's thoughts raced with the implications of their actions. He had never felt such a profound connection with another person, and the realization left him both exhilarated and unnerved. Marianne, too, seemed to grapple with the intensity of their shared moment, her eyes wide with surprise and wonder.

Marianne blinked, her heart racing wildly in the aftermath of their entanglement. For a moment, the world beyond the carriage faded away, leaving only the warmth of Edward's breath mingling with her own. But as the silence enveloped them, doubt crept in, shattering the spell. She pulled back slightly, her cheeks flushed, and looked into his eyes with a mixture of confusion and curiosity.

"You've been with a man before?" Edward asked, his tone direct, betraying none of the hesitation that might have gripped another in such a delicate moment.

Marianne's voice trembled slightly, less accusatory and more inquisitive than she had intended. "Yes," she confessed honestly, a flicker of vulnerability crossing her features. "With a farmer's son I believed I would marry. He died in an accident." The words hung in the air, heavy with unspoken emotions, and she felt a rush of memories flood back—the laughter, the dreams, and the abrupt loss that had shaped her life.

Edward stared at her, his deep green eyes widening in surprise. She was full of surprises, layers of complexity unfurling before him like the petals of a blooming flower, revealing a depth he had not anticipated. The revelation shifted the dynamic between them, igniting a spark of intrigue that both thrilled and unnerved him.

The words hung in the air between them, charged with a mixture of vulnerability and defiance. Her hazel eyes searched Edward's face, seeking answers to questions she hadn't even fully formed in her own mind.

"Why did you believe you could take liberty with me?" she asked, her voice steady despite the turmoil roiling within her. Her fingers, betraying her calm facade, unconsciously fidgeted with the soft fabric of her dress, twisting it nervously as if it could somehow shield her from the weight of his gaze. "Was it because of my station?" The question hung in the air, a challenge laced with vulnerability, as she sought to unveil the truth behind his audacity.

The weight of societal expectations pressed down upon her, threatening to suffocate the spark of connection she had felt moments ago. Marianne's heart raced, torn between the desire to believe in the authenticity of their shared moment and the fear that she was merely a pawn in some greater game of the aristocracy.

Edward, momentarily lost in the haze of the moment, blinked as if awakening from a delightful dream. A roguish smile spread across his face, one that hinted at the devil-may-care charm he was known for, yet something softened in his expression. "I must apologize, Miss Connelly," he said, his tone playful but sincere. "Your *beauty* simply overtook me. I couldn't help myself."

Marianne raised an eyebrow, a teasing smile tugging at her lips despite the uncertainty swirling within her. "A simple beauty spell, is it? *Your* beauty overcame me as well," she retorted, and continued, "What would society say if they knew that a notorious rake and a mere lady's maid could be so easily enchanted?"

His chuckle echoed within the carriage, easing the tension that had built up around their intimate moment. "Ah, but darling Marianne, society is so often mistaken. They would never believe I could be so easily beguiled by a woman of substance and wit. I would be utterly scandalized! What sort of reputation would that bestow upon me?"

Despite herself, Marianne laughed again, which lightened the atmosphere further. Yet beneath her amusement lay a nervous fluttering, a sensation that dared to rise up amidst her growing affection for him. "You are quite the scoundrel, my lord. To kiss and take what is not yours without thought of consequence. And what other thrills have you foolishly pursued?"

"Thrill is my stock in trade," he confessed, leaning back against the carriage seat with an exaggerated sigh. "I have trifled with the hearts of countless young ladies, indulged in the finest wines, and leaped from rooftops in the name of adventure. But never have I —" he raised an eyebrow, slyly glancing at her "—found myself snared by a lady's maid."

Marianne opened her mouth in mock disbelief, her laughter punctuating the gravity of the moment. "You boast of your conquests, yet here you are, lamenting your fate with none other than a mere lady's maid."

"Ah, but in this instance," he leaned closer, his voice theatrical, "you are no mere lady's maid. You are a spirited enchantress who has captured my attention against all reason." His gaze intensified, eyes gleaming with a fervent light, drawing Marianne in deeper.

"Yet you imply I am at fault for this entanglement," Marianne smirked, although the teasing lilt in her tone barely concealed the tornado of emotions swirling within her.

"Fault?" He let out a breathless laugh and shifted his weight playfully, closing the distance again. "I would never blame you for such enchanting beauty. You're the one who has me questioning the very core of my nature."

There it was, that wicked twist of charm that had so often captivated the ladies of the ton, yet somehow felt different in this moment. Marianne's heart skipped a beat, drawn closer by a tension that was both electric and entirely unfamiliar.

Edward's thoughts were interrupted by the sudden jolt of the carriage, as it came to an abrupt halt. The spell between them was broken, and they found themselves thrust back into the reality of their situation. With a mixture of reluctance and curiosity, they peered out the window, seeking an explanation for their unexpected stop.

Outside, the dimly lit streets of London were alive with activity, as revelers spilled out of nearby taverns and theaters. The carriage had come to a stop in front of a bustling inn, its glowing windows casting a warm, inviting light onto the cobblestone street. As Edward and Marianne exchanged puzzled glances, the carriage door swung open, revealing the smiling face of the coachman.

"Apologies for the delay, milord, milady," he said, tipping his hat in their direction. "But it seems we've run into a bit of a predicament. The horses have grown weary, and they'll need a spell to rest before we can continue on our journey."

Edward and Marianne shared a look of concern, acutely aware of the potential consequences of their prolonged absence. And yet, as they surveyed the lively scene before them, a sense of opportunity began to take hold. Perhaps this unexpected pause in their journey was a chance to explore the possibilities of their newfound connection, free from the constraints of society and the expectations that had long defined their lives.

As the carriage came to an abrupt halt, Edward's eyes widened in recognition of the familiar figures approaching. His heart pounded in his chest as he realized the precarious situation they found themselves in – being seen with Marianne could ignite a scandal that would tarnish both their reputations.

Turning to Marianne, his expression was a mixture of urgency and reassurance. "Quick, you must duck down and conceal yourself," he whispered, his voice low and intense. "If we're seen together, the consequences could be disastrous."

Marianne's eyes widened, but she nodded in understanding, swiftly lowering herself onto the carriage floor and pulling a heavy cloak over her form. Her heart raced with a mixture of excitement and apprehension, the thrill of their adventure now tinged with the weight of potential scandal.

Edward took a deep breath, steeling himself for the encounter ahead. He straightened his posture and adjusted his cravat, donning the mask of nonchalance that had served him well in countless social situations.

As the group of gentlemen approached, Edward plastered a charming smile on his face and leaned casually against the carriage door. "Ah, gentlemen!" he called out, his voice rich with feigned surprise. "What an unexpected pleasure to encounter you on this fine evening."

The men exchanged curious glances, their eyes darting toward the carriage with undisguised curiosity. One of them, a portly gentleman with a ruddy complexion, stepped forward with a knowing grin.

"Lord Grey," he greeted, his tone laced with mischief. "We couldn't help but notice your carriage and thought to inquire if you might be in need of assistance."

Edward let out a hearty chuckle, his eyes twinkling with mirth. "Assistance? Nonsense, my good man! I assure you, everything is quite in order." He paused, allowing a roguish grin to spread across his features. "Merely enjoying a leisurely evening ride, as any gentleman is wont to do."

The men exchanged skeptical glances, their curiosity piqued by Edward's evasive response. One of them, a lanky fellow with a hawkish nose, leaned in conspiratorially.

"Come now, Grey," he prodded, his voice low and conspiratorial. "We all know your reputation for dalliances. Surely there's no need for secrecy among friends."

Edward's smile never faltered, though a flicker of unease passed through his eyes. He knew he needed to tread carefully, lest their suspicions grow. With a dismissive wave of his hand, he let out another boisterous laugh.

"Gentlemen, I assure you, your imaginations are running wild," he chided, his tone light and playful. "But if you must know, I was merely seeking a moment of solitude away from the prying eyes of the ton. A man needs his privacy, after all."

The men exchanged skeptical glances, but Edward's charm seemed to disarm their suspicions, at least for the moment. The portly gentleman clapped him on the shoulder, a jovial grin spreading across his face.

"Very well, Grey," he conceded with a wink. "We shan't pry any further. But do be careful – the gossips of London have eyes and ears everywhere."

With a chorus of laughter and well-wishes, the group of gentlemen bid Edward farewell and continued on their way, their curiosity temporarily sated. As their footsteps faded into the distance, Edward let out a sigh of relief, his shoulders visibly relaxing.

Turning back to the carriage, he rapped lightly on the door. "It's safe now, Marianne," he called out softly. "They've gone."

Slowly, Marianne emerged from her hiding place, her cheeks flushed with a mixture of excitement and embarrassment. She smoothed her skirts and met Edward's gaze, her hazel eyes dancing with a newfound sense of mischief.

"That was a close call," she murmured, her voice tinged with amusement. "You handled them remarkably well, Lord Grey."

Edward chuckled, his rakish charm resurfacing as he offered her a roguish wink. "Years of practice, my dear," he quipped. "Though I must admit, the thrill of evading prying eyes is quite invigorating."

As they settled back into the carriage, a charged silence fell between them, the weight of their dalliance lingering in the air. Edward found himself captivated by Marianne's spirit, her quick wit and daring nature igniting a spark within him that he hadn't felt in years. The longer he remained in her company, the stronger his desire to feel her against him again grew, to draw her into an embrace once more and savor the flavor of her flesh.

As the carriage resumed its journey, a comfortable silence settled between them once more. Edward found himself reflecting on the events of the evening, his admiration for Marianne growing with each passing moment.

He had always prided himself on his ability to charm and seduce, but Marianne's quick thinking and unwavering poise had left him in awe. She was more than just a lady's maid – she was a woman of substance, a kindred spirit who challenged him in ways he had never anticipated.

Marianne, too, found herself reevaluating her perceptions of Edward. Beneath the veneer of the notorious rake lay a man yearning for something more, a depth of character that resonated with her own desires for authenticity.

As their gazes met once more, a silent understanding passed between them – a recognition that their unexpected adventure had forged a bond that transcended the boundaries of their respective stations.

"Miss Connelly," Edward said, clearing his throat, his voice tinged with a hint of nervousness that surprised even himself. He shifted his weight, suddenly aware of the rapid beating of his heart. "Would you be interested in—"

"No," Marianne said to the quick, cutting him off with a firmness that belied the flutter in her stomach. She knew precisely what he was about to ask, and she wasn't interested in becoming his mistress. While other women in service would jump at the chance of becoming a wealthy man's bedmate, Marianne wanted more for herself. The very thought of it sent a shiver of indignation down her spine. She lifted her chin, meeting his gaze with unwavering resolve, determined not to let her true feelings show. The air between them crackled with unspoken tension, a mixture of attraction and defiance that threatened to overwhelm them both.

"You will be discreet then?" Edward asked gently, his voice barely above a whisper. His emerald eyes searched her face, a flicker of concern passing through them despite his attempt at nonchalance.

Marianne swallowed her tears, forcing them back with every ounce of willpower she possessed. Her throat constricted painfully as she met his gaze, her own eyes shimmering with unshed emotion. "Yes, my lord," she managed to reply, her voice steady despite the tempest raging within her heart. The words tasted bitter on her tongue, a stark reminder of the vast chasm between their stations.

The carriage entered the Woodfeld Estate, with its long driveway surrounded by rows of trees. When the carriage rounded a bend, Edward's breath caught in his throat. Up ahead, a familiar figure stood at the entrance, her silhouette unmistakable in the flickering gaslight. She was standing with her parents, the Viscount and Viscountess of Woodfeld.

It was Lady Emily Percy, her expression a mix of confusion and concern as she watched the carriage approach.

Edward exchanged a worried glance with Marianne, the weight of their predicament settling upon them once more. They had been discovered, and the consequences of their daring escapade were about to unfold.

CHAPTER NINE
the arrival at woodfeld estate

As Edward alighted from the carriage, he turned and extended a hand to help Marianne disembark, his playful exuberance very much intact. However, the moment his eyes aligned with hers, he felt a jolt of reality pierce his delight. Their surroundings shifted as they caught sight of Lady Emily standing elegantly in the doorway—a regal figure framed by the soft glow spilling from within the mansion. The anticipation on her face twisted with discontent, her arms crossed with the kind of poise that belied the storm brewing behind her expressive blue eyes.

Marianne faltered in her step, heart racing as a flicker of panic ignited within her. As she locked eyes with Lady Emily, a myriad of emotions clashed within her—a tumult of friendship, loyalty, and the unsettling realization of the absurdity of the night's adventure. *How would she face Lady Emily after infringing upon the very boundaries they had both held dear?*

Once more Edward turned, pulling her from her reverie with a comical grin as he stood back, still unaware of the tension he had just stepped into. He reached for Marianne's arm, but his gaze remained transfixed on Lady Emily, light laughter fading into a more serious tone. "Never fear, darling! We've only just begun this adventure!"

However, his joviality crumbled in the weight of Lady Emily's stare, her lips pursed in disapproval, and nothing within him prepared him for the cold reality she presented.

"Ah, my lord," she began, an eyebrow raised incredulously. "Do tell us how your most audacious evening transpired." There was a glimmer of amusement in her eyes, but it was quickly overshadowed by the sharpness of her complement.

Edward, ever the charmer, seized the moment to smooth over the tension. "It was quite a whirlwind, I assure you," he declared, his grin returning as he exaggerated how he was overcoming obstacles, fabricating tales of daring dilemmas and narrow escapes to embellish the unfolding farce.

Marianne struggled against the rising tide of laughter, a muffled giggle escaping her lips despite the precariousness of their situation. She watched as Edward spun an elaborate narrative about thrilling escapades and the reckless allure of forbidden adventures, each embellishment only weaving the tangled web of misunderstandings deeper.

To her surprise, Lady Emily's skepticism deepened. "Oh? Thrilling adventures, is it?" Her arms crossed tighter, skepticism lacing her tone. "Pray tell, just how *thrilling* was this rendezvous—you gallivanting about London while I remained here waiting, bathed in your absence?"

Edward's next witty retort caught in his throat; the flicker of mirth on his face extinguished, replaced by an uncertain understanding of the implications. As he stepped forward, lightheartedness giving way to intrigue, he struggled against the tide of emotions washing over her. "I meant no harm, Lady Emily. The night simply unfolded in—"

"I do not wish to hear your explanations," she interjected firmly, her composure reaffirmed through sheer will. "You found your adventure, Lord Grey. So now please, take your leave."

A stillness fell over the trio. The air thickened with unspoken words and the feelings that had begun bubbling just beneath the surface. Edward's expression shifted from confusion to concern, his emerald gaze searching Emily's face, seeking the person he had thought he knew. When the finality settled into her tone, it felt like an echo of a tone he had never heard before from her.

Edward settled back, caught in an unexpected moment of realization before his internal confusion wrestled its way to the forefront. He dared not set eyes on the woman who brought on such uncertainty, so he decided to keep his focus on Lady Emily.

Marianne's heart twisted as she witnessed the turmoil rising in her friend and Lord Grey's sudden disinterest; she internally lamented the circumstances that had led them here. Yet, caught in the throes of doubt, she felt positioned as an outsider within this tempest swirling about the two.

It was then that the looming figure of the Viscount of Woodfeld stepped into the scene. "Not so fast, Grey," he declared, the fatherly authority in his voice slicing through the tension. Both Lady Emily and Edward turned to face him, surprise mingling with unease. "What adventure could you possibly entail, Grey? Might there be something long-term in the works?" he inquired, studying the two of them now puzzled and caught off-kilter.

Marianne felt as if the room contracted around her as the Viscount's gaze settled on her imperceptibly, brow furrowing. With an awkward glance exchanged, he dismissed her to the servant's quarters. Reluctance bubbled within her, but knowing she'd only muddle things further, she took a step back and retreated.

From the tableau left behind, Edward bowed slightly, hiding the breadth of uncertainty beneath a veneer of grace. "If that is what you wish, my lord," he said, attempting to adhere to the shifting ground beneath him while pretending a calm facade.

The Viscount escorted the Earl into his study with his daughter following closely behind.

Emily watched her father close the door behind them when her jealousy and frustration boiled just below the surface, thick and suffocating. The exciting promise of the night, which had first bloomed in her chest, now left her feeling isolated within the tension building between herself and Edward.

"Perhaps you might listen to me," she continued, her chin tilted defiantly. "The truth is I sought adventure tonight too... I devised the dare, you see. Clearly, I meant to ensnare Lord Grey, with a faux elopement."

"I see," the Viscount replied carefully, his hand stroking his chin thoughtfully. "And you, my lord? What role did you play in this amusing adventure?"

Edward stood still, feeling the weight of the moment pressing against his chest. "I was a willing participant, to be sure. If it is any consolation, it was only meant to be in jest." Yet the words sounded hollow even to him as the tumult of feelings converged within, trapping him beneath an invisible weight.

The Viscount stood silent for a moment then walked over to the window and pretended to look outside. His eyes sharpened, tracing the contours of the tension thickening. "It appears, then, a *marriage* shall be the only acceptable resolution to your evening's antics," he stated with neither malice nor fervor, just an infusion of pragmatic resolve settling beneath his words.

Edward felt overwhelmed. He ran a hand through his hair, the reality of the situation swirling into confusion and fear. The tension was palpable, thickening in the air between them.

And yet, amid the thrumming discord, there was also the stirrings of something irresistibly hook-laden—a dreadful awareness that both Lord Grey and Lady Emily had dressed the evening in adventure, only to unintentionally pique an unexpected entanglement they both found themselves trapped within.

AS MARIANNE MADE her way toward her modest room, the echoes of the evening lingered in her mind, a mixture of laughter, confusion, and unexpected connections. She was still reeling from the chaotic night spent in the company of Lord Grey. Surely, no one had expected it would lead to so much tumult—a mistaken identity, a tavern rendezvous, a curious kiss leading to pleasure, and now, the looming specter of a marriage contract binding Lord Grey to her employer.

What will become of me? she mused, her steps slowing as the weight of uncertainty fell heavy on her heart. Lady Emily's daring escapade had not only entangled them all in a web of scandal but had also trapped Edward in a gilded cage of societal expectations. The Viscount would exploit his daughter's whims to secure an advantageous match, and from the moment she had witnessed their flirtations, Marianne had feared the outcome.

The gnawing fear of the repercussions tightened around her chest. *What does it mean for me, if Lord Grey is truly forfeited as a husband? How could I possibly serve them when the temptation of bedding Lord Grey again would always loom like clouds?* She shuddered, realizing that her own connection to the notorious rake could cast shadows on her aspirations for independence—an unsettling prospect as she prepared for bed.

Once the vows were exchanged and Lord Grey had taken Lady Emily as his wife, Marianne's position would be utterly untenable. What reason could Lady Emily possibly have for retaining her services?

The night had felt long and exhausting, filled with laughter that now felt distant. In her modest quarters, she disrobed slowly, removed paths of excitement from her skin like shedding a snake's skin layer by layer. Her undergarments were wet and she discarded them immediately. Just as she unclasped her gown, the door swung open without warning.

Lady Emily stormed in, her expression a tempest of frustration and jealousy that startled Marianne from the calm her private sanctuary offered. "Marianne!" she exclaimed, her eyes flashing. "You had *no right* to get lost in the chaos while I—" She faltered, struggling to contain the emotion that rose in her throat. "Do you not understand? He was supposed to share this adventure with me!"

Marianne pulled her gown closer, heart thumping boldly in her chest as she met Emily's gaze. "I wasn't lost, Lady Emily. I was... trying to keep things from spiraling further out of control." Her voice softened, attempting to soothe the agitated air surrounding them. "You know as well as I do that the consequences of the night's follies do not belong solely to you—it includes me, too."

Emily's frustration ebbed slightly, and she paced the room, her demeanor shifting from hostility to introspection. "It wasn't how I wanted it to happen. A marriage with Lord Grey should be based on love, not a manipulation of circumstance."

"So, it is done?" Marianne asked, feeling her throat close up.

Lady Emily dug her slipper into the floor, "Yes, my father demanded it."

"Congratulations," Marianne replied, her tone calm yet tinged with sadness. "We bear the weight of the choices we've made. But perhaps, in time, this unexpected pairing may bring the two of you something genuine... despite the circumstances."

"Do you truly believe that?" Emily asked, her voice carrying a note of skepticism. "How can I trust my heart won't be trapped by this forced arrangement?"

"Love finds a way in the most unexpected places," Marianne assured, though her own heart quivered with uncertainty. "We both know that, even in the most unlikeliest of circumstances, there's a path forward. This could lead to something profound for you both. Lord Grey has shown depths beyond his reputation..."

Lady Emily turned, her gaze piercing through Marianne. "How do you know this?"

Marianne's heart raced as she grappled with the weight of her unspoken secret. The memory of Edward's kiss lingered on her lips, a bittersweet reminder of the connection they had shared. But as she gazed upon Lady Emily's troubled countenance, she knew that revealing such a truth would only serve to deepen the rift between them.

"My lady," Marianne began, her voice soft yet firm, "I assure you, there is nothing to be jealous of. Lord Grey spoke of you with the utmost admiration throughout our unexpected adventure."

Lady Emily's eyes narrowed, searching Marianne's face for any hint of deception. "Did he truly? Then why did he not return to me immediately upon realizing his mistake?"

Marianne took a steadying breath, carefully choosing her words. "My lady, you must understand the delicate nature of the situation. We found ourselves in a tavern surrounded by prying eyes and wagging tongues. To have rushed back without a proper explanation would have only fueled the fires of gossip."

She stepped closer to Lady Emily, her voice dropping to a conspiratorial whisper. "In truth, I believe I have saved you from certain ruin. Think of it, my lady. No one knows that this engagement was forced. You have the opportunity to shape the narrative as you see fit."

Lady Emily's brow furrowed as she contemplated Marianne's words. "What do you mean?"

"Consider this," Marianne continued, a hint of excitement creeping into her voice. "You can present this engagement as a romantic gesture, orchestrated by Lord Grey himself. A dashing proposal, perhaps? One that swept you off your feet and left you with no choice but to accept."

A glimmer of intrigue sparked in Lady Emily's eyes. "Go on," she urged, her earlier hostility giving way to curiosity.

Marianne, emboldened by her lady's interest, pressed on. "Imagine the tale we could weave. Lord Grey, overcome by his affections, arranging a clandestine meeting in a moonlit garden. He confesses his undying love, goes down on one knee, and presents you with a ring that has been in his family for generations."

Lady Emily's lips curled into a small smile, clearly captivated by the romantic picture Marianne was painting. "It does sound rather dashing, doesn't it?"

"Indeed, it does," Marianne agreed, her heart lightening at the sight of her lady's improved mood. "And who would dare question such a romantic tale? It would be the talk of the ton for seasons to come."

Lady Emily sank onto the edge of Marianne's bed, her fingers absently toying with the fabric of her gown. "But what of the truth? What of my father's involvement?"

Marianne knelt before her, taking Lady Emily's hands in her own. "My lady, in matters of the heart, the truth is often what we choose it to be. Your father's involvement need not be known beyond these walls. To the world, this can be a love match of the highest order."

For a moment, Lady Emily's eyes shone with the possibilities Marianne had presented. But then, like a cloud passing over the sun, doubt crept back into her expression. "And what of Lord Grey? Will he play along with this charade?"

Marianne hesitated, recalling Edward's charm and quick wit. "I believe Lord Grey to be a man of great resourcefulness. If approached with this plan, I have no doubt he would rise to the occasion. After all, it would save his reputation as much as yours."

Lady Emily nodded slowly, her earlier jealousy and hesitation giving way to a tentative calm. "Perhaps you are right, Marianne. Perhaps this is not the disaster I initially feared."

Marianne squeezed her lady's hands gently. "It need not be a disaster at all, my lady. With careful planning and a united front, this could be the beginning of a grand romance."

A small laugh escaped Lady Emily's lips. "A grand romance indeed. Who would have thought my little dare would lead to this?"

Marianne smiled, relieved to see her lady's spirits lifting. "Life often takes us down unexpected paths, my lady. It is up to us to make the best of the journey."

Lady Emily stood, smoothing out her gown. "You are right, of course. Thank you, Marianne. Your wisdom and quick thinking may have saved us all from a most unfortunate scandal."

As Lady Emily made her way to the door, she paused, turning back to Marianne with a hint of her earlier mischief in her eyes. "I must say, for someone who claims to have had such an uneventful night, you seem to have gained quite an insight into the Earl's character."

Marianne felt a flush creep up her neck, but she met Lady Emily's gaze steadily. "I merely observed, my lady. It is a skill I have honed in my years of service."

Lady Emily nodded, seemingly satisfied with this explanation. "Well, your observations may prove invaluable in the days to come. We shall need all the insight we can gather if we are to pull off this grand deception."

As the door closed behind Lady Emily, Marianne let out a long, shaky breath. The calm that had settled over her lady was a relief, but Marianne could not shake the feeling that it was merely the eye of the storm. Lady Emily's jealousy and hesitation, though momentarily quelled, still simmered beneath the surface.

Marianne sank onto her bed, her mind whirling with the events of the night and the potential complications that lay ahead. She had managed to smooth Lady Emily's ruffled feathers for now, but how long would this fragile peace last? And what of her own conflicted feelings for Lord Grey?

As she prepared for bed, Marianne found herself both exhausted and exhilarated by the night's adventures. She had played her part well, deflecting suspicion and soothing her lady's wounded pride. But as she closed her eyes, the memory of Edward's kiss haunted her dreams, a bittersweet reminder of what might have been and what could never be.

CHAPTER TEN
the morning after

Sunlight streamed through the large windows of Woodfeld Estate's dining room, casting a warm, golden glow on the elegant furnishings. Fingertip-sized droplets of dew clung to the petals of the delicate flowers arranged in a pristine porcelain vase at the center of the table. The cheerful notes of birdsong floated through the open panes, mixing with the soft clatter of dishes and the gentle hum of conversations as the household staff bustled about, tending to their morning duties.

Lady Emily Percy, resplendent in a gown of soft lavender silk, flitted gracefully around the breakfast table where her parents, the Viscount and Viscountess of Woodfeld, sat awaiting their morning repast. Her demeanor radiated delight, every movement imbued with a rustle of energy that seemed to brighten the very air around her. A glossy ringlet escaped its confines, cascading artlessly over her shoulder, but she paid it no mind, too enraptured by her own joyful anticipation.

"Have you ever seen such glorious weather, Mama? The sun shines as if it knows today is a day of momentous news!" Emily's voice chimed like a lovely bell as she nestled herself into her seat, excitement evident in her animated gestures.

"A lovely morning indeed, my dear," her mother replied, a smile tugging at her lips. The Viscountess regarded her daughter with a mixture of fondness and curiosity. "And what, may I ask, has you so taken with joy?"

Before Emily could respond, the dining room doors flung open with unexpected zeal, and Miss Beatrice Caldwell rushed in, her presence as vivacious as the morning sun itself. A flurry of fabric accompanied her energetic entrance, the vivid green of her dress a stark contrast to the pastel hues typically seen amidst the morning gatherings.

"Oh! I beg your pardon for my intrusion!" Beatrice exclaimed, her brown eyes sparkling as she scanned the table before affectionately fixing them on Emily. "But I simply had to know if it is true. Miss Pemberton was positively gushing this morning at our gathering, claiming to have overheard the most delightful bit of gossip!"

"Oh, dear heavens! You heard of it too?" Lady Emily's heart flared with joy as she leaned forward, her eyes wide with a mixture of exhilaration and disbelief. "Yes! It is true! Lord Grey and I are to be married!"

The declaration slipped from her lips like a fragile secret shared among friends, although she reveled in the certainty with which she spoke. "Can you believe it? Edward—no, Lord Grey—proposed just last night! It was all so very romantic!" She promptly recounted the tale of their supposed elopement—of midnight strolls beneath the stars, whispered promises, and the serendipitous events that had led to this blossoming engagement.

As she spoke, the dining room transformed into her own personal stage, each word carefully crafted as she spun the elaborate tale.

Her parents listened with rapt attention, sharing glances that oscillated between pride and incredulity.

"Of course, my dear! Your happiness is all that matters," the Viscountess encouraged gently, though her brow knitted slightly as she chose her next words carefully. "But, is it wise to pursue such a fast engagement? The society will surely spin tales."

"Ah, Mama! What of it! What is life without a little drama?" Lady Emily replied, the thrill bubbling within her chest as she dismissed her mother's cautionary tone with a flick of her wrist. "Such tales serve only to add to the romance! As if prying eyes could ever dampen the spirit of a true love!"

The staff moved quietly through the room, placing dishes before the family while exchanging glances that revealed their loyalty to Emily. Each footman and maid felt the infectious energy radiating from their lady. A smile tugged at the lips of the head maid, who silently cheered for Lady Emily as she padded about with the grace of an artist, preparing the canvas of her life to be painted brighter than ever.

"Such splendid news!" Miss Caldwell interjected, clasping her hands before her chest, clearly enraptured by Emily's joy. "I shall be the first to tell everyone—I cannot wait to see their faces when they learn the news!"

"Oh, Beatrice, do not spoil it! I want my announcement to come as a delightful surprise—let the soirée tonight be our grand reveal!" Lady Emily's eyes twinkled mischievously, relishing the thought of orchestrating a veritable fairy tale most anticipated by their circle.

"You mean the soirée where you dance with every eligible bachelor? I daresay some will be positively shattered!" Beatrice laughed, admiring the spark of rebellion evident in Emily's schemes.

At that moment, the ambiance shifted as a footman discreetly entered to refill their cups, the warm aroma of fresh tea wafting through the air. Edward's enthrallment with Lady Emily was the talk of the household; even the servants had taken to conspiring over their future. As he poured the tea, their gazes met, and he exchanged a knowing smile with Lady Emily, wherein lay a shared understanding that only served to amplify the excitement thrumming through the heart of the estate.

"Perhaps I shall take it upon myself to arrange a meeting with Lord Grey, to ensure his intentions are honorable," the Viscount said, clearing his throat, though his gaze glimmered with the warmth reserved for his beloved daughter.

"Papa!" Lady Emily's laughter rang out, brightening the dim corners of the room. "What need have you for the formalities when love itself unites us?" Her voice was light, yet within her words lay the vibrant fervor of youthful recklessness—a characteristic that endeared her to many and caused her parents great concern all at once.

"I shall keep watch on his words, my dear," he replied with mock gravitas, though the curve of his lips revealed that he relished the unfolding drama. A soft chuckle rippled through the surrounding staff, who marveled at the playful banter weaving past the fine linens of the breakfast table.

As conversation resumed, Lady Emily returned to recounting her imagined future with the Earl of Grey, breathing life into plans of future soirées and genteel family gatherings. Her ardor sparkled with optimism, weaving dreams of a beautiful life ahead—a life filled with tender glances and romantic rendezvous amid the whispers of the ton.

In this special moment, she felt unstoppable; balanced in the calm of life's wild wind, she gave in to love's excited shaking as dawn lit up the start of a thrilling new part. Through the laughter around her, she clung to her dreams, letting hope cover society's growing demands, thinking she had really made her own storybook ending.

DOWNSTAIRS in the heart of Woodfeld Estate, the dining room buzzed with the laughter and chatter of servants gathered at the long table, piping hot plates of breakfast set before them. In the kitchen, bakers and cooks exchanged warmth and friendliness, punctuated by the scent of freshly baked bread mingled with the delicate aroma of soft scrambled eggs. But while the atmosphere thrummed with delightful energy, Marianne Connelly could scarcely enjoy a single morsel. She feigned a smile at the exuberance of her fellow staff, though beneath her outwardly pleasant demeanor brewed a tumultuous storm of conflicting emotions.

A fellow maid clapped her hands together, her silver bracelets jingling cheerfully. "Did you hear the news?" she said, practically bouncing in her seat. "Lady Emily is to be wed to Lord Grey! It's a love story straight out of a novel!"

Marianne nodded, hearing the familiar jingle of joy around her, yet her heart felt like a stone at the very bottom of a well. She forced a smile that didn't quite reach her eyes, the bright glee of her colleagues ringing painfully hollow against the weight of her bittersweet emotions. Joy for her friend, yes, but also a deep emptiness that clawed at her chest. Such a notion as a "love story" seemed cruelly mocking, particularly when it stirred the unacknowledged feelings she had harbored for the very man who now promised to sweep Lady Emily away. Each cheerful voice filled her with a jab of jealousy, not at Emily for the engagement but at herself for the foolish dreams she had dared to entertain.

The conversation buzzed around her in happy disbelief, her friends excitedly imagining the splendor of an engagement party, while Marianne stared at her uneaten food. The ordinary noise of dishes and cheerful chatter offered no comfort, only intensifying the pain inside her. She admired Lady Emily's lively dreams and strong belief in true love, while considering the slim chance that those same dreams would never be part of her own life—the life of a lady's maid, always overshadowed by the truths of social class and expectation.

LATER THAT AFTERNOON, Lady Emily bustled around her room, her voice ringing with excitement as she paced like a caged bird finally set free. "Oh, Marianne! Can you imagine? An announcement to the ton! Just think of it! My name in the papers as the future Countess of Grey!" Her eyes sparkled with a mix of joy and determination, a vision of happiness in which marrying Edward seemed to promise an existence fabricated from the pages of a romantic novel.

Marianne clutched a brush in her hand, her eyes reflecting concern rather than the shared exhilaration radiating from her friend. She took in her surroundings, the luxurious fabrics draping the walls and the delicate porcelain laid lovingly on every surface, yet found herself not swept up in the delight but ensnared by a growing apprehension.

"Lady Emily," she interjected gently, her voice steady yet filled with an uncharacteristic hesitance. The air around them felt charged with the urgency of her words. "It's not ... not a mere announcement. Have you considered the implications of such a public declaration?" Her heart raced as she stepped closer, willing the tension to be replaced by understanding.

Lady Emily waved a dismissive hand, her laughter ringing like the tinkle of silver coins. "Nonsense! We're in the age of romance! Every lady dreams of a grand wedding, and you must indulge me! Besides, once the announcement splashes across Hightown, the buzz will be undeniable! It'll be exciting! A soirée, a dance, an evening filled with notable company—it will be the grandest celebration of my life!"

Marianne frowned, her spirit half-heartedly lifting to Lady Emily's dazzling enthusiasm for a fleeting moment, before the weight of reality pulled it back down. "But forcing this marriage seems only to court disaster," she argued, stepping forward to grab Lady Emily's wrist, the playful glimmer of her friend's planning dimmed under Marianne's earnest gaze. "You mustn't rush into this. Bound as you will be, are you truly willing to lose your own will to this engagement?"

"Why must you be so serious?" Lady Emily glanced back, her eyes widening with indignation, but perhaps ... a flicker of doubt hid beneath her bold facade. "This is what I have always wanted! The thrill of a fairy tale! The chatter of the town! Envy! Love?"

Marianne sighed, her expression softening but resolute. "But celebrity fades, Lady Emily. Consider the reality of life as Lady Grey. Your happiness cannot only dwell in dreams and praises... What of your soul? What of what drives you? You deserve a love born of yearning and desire—something genuine that nourishes your heart, not a mere spectacle for the ton."

As Lady Emily's fervor began to wane, her brow furrowing, Marianne pressed on, a hopeful hope nestled deep within her earnestness. "Think of what it means to be committed to someone. A decision made this soon might bind you to Lord Grey without discovering what it means to truly feel for one another."

"I don't want to discuss this," Lady Emily muttered, her tone tingeing dangerously close to frustration, though she visibly fought against her growing reluctance. "The world is watching. I just want to revel in this dream."

Marianne opened her mouth, searching her thoughts for just the right words, the ones that would resonate with her, coaxing her to reconsider. But before she could gather them, the sound of the door swinging open interrupted them.

"Your Ladyship!" A footman rushed in, breathless and filled with rumors of progress. "Lady Emily, the staff has already prepared the announcements more than once for you. We are ready to send your news with all due haste!"

"See?" Emily proclaimed, her brightness renewed. "It is meant to be! The whole house witnesses the unfolding — they believe in us!"

Deep down, Marianne's heart sank again, the notion of "the whole house" filling her with dread. She watched as her friend's face lit with anticipation, an eagerness taking hold like a twisted vine, wrapping around every sensible thought, binding her to the whims of the wider world.

"Lady Emily…" she began, yet the urgency in her friend's eyes silenced her, its fervor unwilling to entertain a moment's doubt.

"Tomorrow, a grand soirée," Lady Emily declared, her voice rising against the walls of the room, recreating past visions filled with beauty and love. "Every guest we could entrust, sprinkled with laughter, delightful music, and of course, they'll toast to my engagement."

Marianne watched her with eyes of both warmth and apprehension. As her friend sketched the exhilarating details of the ball upon parchment paper, societal norms began to trap her further in the excitement—a celebration steeped in tradition, yet one that echoed with echoes of foreboding.

CHAPTER ELEVEN
the ton's response

The elegant ballroom of the Mayfair estate buzzed with the infectious excitement of its guests. Crystal chandeliers sparkled overhead, illuminating a sea of sumptuous silks and extravagant gowns where laughter and well-wishes mingled with the soft strains of a string quartet. Lady Emily Percy, radiant in her pale lavender gown—a perfect complement to her expressive blue eyes—was the focal point of every whispered conversation.

"Have you heard?" gushed Miss Beatrice Caldwell, gripping the arm of her fellow debutante with exaggerated fervor. "Lady Emily has succeeded where many have failed! Engaged to the Earl of Grey himself! It's positively marvelous!"

Coos and cheers erupted around Emily as her friends enveloped her in a circle of delight. Their expressions, painted with envy and admiration, became a tapestry of emotions that pulsed through the room.

"Do tell us how you managed it, Emily!" a lady exclaimed, her wide eyes drinking in the details as though they were the very essence of excitement.

Emily giggled, her cheeks flushed with a blend of pride and mirth. "Oh, really, it was merely a matter of courage and—" she fluffed her skirts with a flourish, "charm."

"Charm?" chimed in another friend, her voice rich with mock incredulity. "You practically ensnared him! Ladies, she's now officially captured London's most eligible bachelor!"

Another chorus of appreciative gasps rose in the air, echoing the festivities that enveloped them. Surrounded by her friends, Emily reveled in the attention, her playful spirit twinkling in the glittering air as she basked in the warmth of their adulation.

Across the ballroom, whispers followed every move she made—a cascade of admiration wrapped around her like the delicate lace of her gown. "What a triumph!" exclaimed a seasoned matron while tucking a strand of hair behind her ear, her words dripping with delicious envy. "I hear he might even start courting her more publicly!"

"Only fitting for such a lady—such a spirited, lovely lady," another voice chimed in. "Imagine the soirées! The balls! The jeering suitors snubbed by that wicked rake! How thrilling!"

AT THE EDGE of the gathering, Marianne stood near the flowering archway that led to the garden, observing the joyous atmosphere with a practiced smile plastered over her features. The vivid colors of the evening juxtaposed sharply against the somber thoughts swirling in her mind. Beneath the jubilant chatter and the clinking of glasses, a heavyweight gripped her, tightening around her heart like a vice.

She watched Lady Emily glow at the center of her admirers, laughter spilling from her lips, enchanting everyone around her. Yet as the echoes of fervent congratulations danced around her, Marianne felt like a shadow lurking on the fringes of vivid light. In this moment of unrestrained joy, she wrestled with feelings that felt foreign—all-consuming and haunting.

Each excited exclamation from the throngs of well-wishers felt like a stab to her heart. The servants bustling about the room exuded an infectious happiness that only deepened her sense of isolation. They prepared for their mistress's celebration, cheerfully exchanging compliments about the young nobleman who was, apparently, more than mere rumor now.

"Her ladyship is more deserving than anyone to capture the attention of such a fine gentleman," one footman remarked, his voice buoyant. "It's enough to send the rest of us hiding her lace in the wardrobe!"

"We must not keep her from enjoying every moment," another maid replied. "It is rare to find an engagement that holds such promise!"

Marianne's heart ached at their happiness. She felt a duality that seeped into her bones—the collective elation in the air clashed ominously with her realities. She wanted to smile along with the others, to join in their joy for Emily's impending marriage, but the truth echoed louder in her mind—her own secret affections for Lord Grey, an affliction that felt heavy like a shroud.

With each congratulatory explosion from the people around her, Marianne found herself retreating deeper into her contemplations. Watching her lady transform into the center of attention buried the unfulfilled dreams she had quietly nurtured.

It felt as if she had become a mere spectator in the grand play of society, swaddled in the melancholy that followed.

"Don't let it chain you, Marianne. Put your feelings aside," she whispered to herself, clenching her hands nervously. Her lips quirked into a smile that was more farce than genuine cheer. She tried to imagine the warmth of Lady Emily's elation wrapping around her like a shawl, but it transformed instead into a ghostly echo, leaving her feeling only the chill of loneliness.

Yet the certainty remained, stark and unyielding: Emily's happiness must come first. "What is a moment of discomfort compared to her joy?" she countered her own feelings, reminding herself of her duty to her lady above all else. Thus, she resolved to be supportive, casting her own heartache to the shadows, like a secret tethered within her as she wallowed in the shadows of another's triumph.

"Miss Connelly? Are you lost in thought?" A soft voice disrupted her reverie, and she turned to find one of the maids regarding her with concern. "You ought to be with the other ladies, celebrating."

Marianne chuckled lightly, shaking her head. "No, I'm merely appreciating the festivities from up close," she replied, eager to dispel the weight of her emotions.

The maid's face broke into a sympathetic smile. "You must not forget your place as her lady's maid. You will surely be elevated and brought into Grey Manor and household. We are all part of this happiness!"

Marianne only nodded as the maid flitted away to join the party, and with that, her resolve wrapped itself tighter around her heart, reminding herself that these moments were not meant for her. She had seen countless engagements, countless loves bloom like flowers, and countless heartbreaks buried like weeds beneath the earth. Love stories were written for others, not for her.

But as she lingered on the outskirts, the briefest flickering of envy swept through her heart. Ever the diligent servant, she felt adrift in the tide, watching the swell of happiness bloom around her and wishing for just one petal of joy to land at her feet.

THE DAY of the party arrived with a lively energy that filled Woodfeld Estate, turning its grand halls into a mix of noise and excitement. Servants rushed to and fro, carrying trays laden with dainty pastries and crystal flutes of sparkling wine, as the air buzzed with anticipation for the evening's festivities. In the heart of this whirlwind stood Miss Connelly, her nimble fingers deftly working against the fabric of Lady Emily's exquisite gown as they prepared for the grand event.

"Just a touch more on the ribbon, Marianne. It must be perfect!" Lady Emily exclaimed, her eyes gleaming with delight. The delicate hue of her gown matched the soft flush of her cheeks, framed by brilliant curls that cascaded in intricate waves around her shoulders.

"Indeed, my lady," Marianne replied, forcing a smile even as her heart tugged at the realization of her own feelings. Each tug of the fabric pulled her deeper into silent conflict, and as she adjusted the last of the satin bows, the weight of her emotions bore down heavily.

As Lady Emily admired her reflection, her excitement bubbled over like champagne poised to overflow. "I am to be the darling of the evening," she declared, a triumphant laugh escaping her.

"Imagine! All of London will be abuzz with the news of my engagement!"

Marianne swallowed her bittersweet thoughts, looking at Lady Emily in the mirror. In that moment, her lady radiated confidence, a vibrant bloom in a sea of admirers. Yet, for Marianne, the anticipation brought an aching uncertainty. As she turned to leave the dressing room, cloaked in her modest attire, she felt like a shadow trailing along behind a luminary.

THE FLURRY of guests entering the estate soon enveloped them in a wave of color and sound. Ladies bedecked in extravagant gowns, shimmering silks that flowed like water, and gentlemen in tailored coats appeared as if summoned by magic. Marianne stood just inside the grand hall, a figure watching from the periphery as laughter rolled through the air like a whispering tide.

"Lady Emily! What a vision!" floated through the din as acquaintances and friends rushed to ensconce the lady of the hour with compliments and adulation. Each praise seemed to amplify the energy in the room, lighting her with an iridescent glow that easily ensnared the attention of all around her.

Amid the throng, Marianne prepared trays of refreshments, moving fluidly between guests while donning a mask of practiced cheerfulness. Yet, each clink of teacups and melody of waltzes underscored a profound isolation. The cheerful cheer echoing through the hall contrasted with the emptiness that burgeoned within her chest, a hidden weight no one could see but her.

As the soirée officially began, Marianne's gaze drifted to the ballroom itself, resplendent with opulent decor: lush floral arrangements bursting with color, twinkling lights suspended to mimic stars, and an orchestra that filled the air with rich melodies. Joyful laughter and clinking of glasses melded into a spirited symphony, mesmerizing the guests as they toasted to Lady Emily's good fortune.

"Raise a glass to our lovely bride-to-be!" one voice rang out, prompting an avalanche of glasses lifted high in celebration. Marianne instinctively mirrored their movements, lifting a glass of her own, even as bittersweet tears glistened at the edges of her eyes.

With every shared laugh and glance of admiration directed at Lady Emily, her heart sank further into a shadowy abyss. The happiness shone so brightly in the eyes of others that it obscured the truth lying beneath the surface of her own masked smile. For as Lady Emily triumphed, her own unsung feelings faded further into the background.

Marianne left the first floor to the safety of the upstairs landing that looked over the dance floor and ballroom down below. Other maids joined her, and a few of them tittered from the excitement of the evening.

Then, as the laughter crescendoed, the ballroom doors swung open dramatically, and Lord Edward Grey strolled in, capturing the collective breath of the room. His presence was magnetic, every eye drawn to him as if he was the sun around which their little society revolved. The gentlemen stepped aside, allowing the ladies to flock to him like moths to a flame.

"Lord Grey!" they exclaimed, breathless and eager, extending their hands toward him with practiced grace. Marianne felt a twinge in her heart—a mix of admiration and chagrin—as the sea of soft silk and full skirts surrounded him, his charming smile met with whispers of envy directed toward Lady Emily. She had not laid eyes on him for a fortnight, and her heart fluttered by his sheer existence.

Yet, amid the fluttering ball gowns and sweet compliments tailored just for him, Edward's searching gaze roamed over the guests, scanning faces until, at last, it fell upon a more subdued shadow standing up above him. A spark ignited within him, and a gentle smile unfurled on his lips.

Lord Edward Grey stood at the center of the ballroom, a sea of admirers swirling around him like leaves caught in an autumn breeze. The air was thick with perfume and excitement, the news of his engagement to Lady Emily Percy still fresh on everyone's lips. Yet, as he nodded and smiled at the endless stream of congratulations, his gaze kept drifting up toward the landing where a familiar figure stood in the shadows.

Marianne.

Her presence was like a beacon, drawing his attention even as he tried to focus on the chatter around him. She looked different tonight, her usual vivacity dimmed, replaced by a quiet melancholy that tugged at his heart. Edward found himself yearning to cross the room, to run upstairs, to speak with her, to unravel the mystery of her subdued demeanor.

"Oh, Lord Grey, you must be thrilled!" Lady Worthington gushed, her fan fluttering with excitement. "Lady Emily is such a catch. You'll make a splendid couple!"

Edward forced his attention back to the conversation, summoning a charming smile. "Indeed, Lady Worthington. I count myself fortunate."

But even as the words left his lips, his eyes betrayed him, once again seeking out Marianne. She stood apart from the revelry, her hands clasped tightly before her as she watched the proceedings with a carefully neutral expression. The sight of her, so clearly isolated from the joy that permeated the room, sent a pang through his chest.

How I long to speak with her, he thought, his smile faltering for a moment. *To explain, to understand... to simply be in her presence once more.*

But he dared not approach her, not here, not *now*. The ton was ever-watchful, their appetite for scandal insatiable. Even the slightest hint of impropriety would set tongues wagging, potentially ruining Marianne's reputation and casting a shadow over his impending nuptials.

"Lord Grey, you simply must tell us how you proposed!" Another voice chimed in, pulling him back to the present. "Was it terribly romantic?"

Edward cleared his throat, desperately trying to recall the story they had concocted. "Ah, well, you know how these things go. A moonlit garden, a declaration of undying love..."

As he spun the tale, embellishing it with just enough detail to satisfy his audience, his mind wandered. He remembered instead the night spent with Marianne, the laughter they had shared, the connection that had sparked between them. It felt more real, more vivid than any fabricated proposal could ever be.

The weight of his predicament settled heavily upon his shoulders. He was trapped, caught between duty and desire, between the expectations of society and the longings of his heart. The engagement to Lady Emily had seemed like a lark at first, a bit of mischief to liven up the Season. Now, it felt like a noose tightening around his neck, stealing away his breath and his freedom.

And Marianne... sweet, clever Marianne. She deserved better than to be relegated to the shadows, forced to watch as he played out this charade. Edward's chest tightened as he recalled the spark in her eyes, the quick wit that had both challenged and delighted him. How different things might have been if fate had not conspired to entangle him with Lady Emily.

"You're a lucky man, Grey," Lord Rutherford clapped him on the back, jolting Edward from his reverie. "Lady Emily's quite the prize."

Edward nodded, mustering a weak smile. "Indeed she is."

But as the words left his lips, his gaze once again sought out Marianne. She was moving now, weaving between the guests with a tray of champagne flutes on the upper landing. Even in her role as a servant, she moved with a grace and dignity that outshone many of the ladies present. Edward's heart ached at the sight. His stare caught hers. They shared an acknowledgment as she nodded her head.

I'm a fool, he thought bitterly. *A damned fool who's managed to hurt everyone involved in this mess.*

The pressure of expectation bore down upon him, suffocating in its intensity. He was the Earl of Grey, the most eligible bachelor in London, now betrothed to one of the season's brightest debutantes. It was a match made in heaven, according to the whispers that floated around the room. Yet he felt like a fraud, play-acting at happiness while his true feelings remained locked away, hidden from view.

As the night wore on, Edward found himself growing increasingly restless. The constant flow of well-wishers, the cloying scent of perfume and flowers, the endless repetition of the same conversation – it all began to grate on his nerves. He longed for escape, for a moment of peace away from the prying eyes of society.

But more than anything, he longed to speak with Marianne. To explain himself, to apologize for the mess he had created, to... what? *Declare his feelings? Beg her forgiveness?* He wasn't even sure what he would say if given the chance. All he knew was that the sight of her was slowly tearing him apart.

Yet he remained rooted to his spot, smiling and nodding as guest after guest offered their congratulations. He was Lord Edward Grey, and he had a role to play. No matter how much it pained him, no matter how desperately he wished to break free from the constraints of his position, he knew he must see this through.

As the orchestra struck up another waltz, Edward found himself being pulled onto the dance floor by an eager young debutante. He moved through the steps mechanically, his body going through the motions while his mind remained fixated on Marianne.

She stood at the edge of the balcony now, her eyes following the dancers with a wistful expression. For a brief moment, their gazes met across the span, and Edward felt his heart skip a beat. In that fleeting connection, he saw a reflection of his own turmoil, his own longing.

But then the moment passed, broken by the swirl of dancers and the constant chatter of the ton. Edward turned his attention back to his partner, forcing a smile as he continued the dance. Yet inside, his heart ached with the weight of unspoken words and unfulfilled desires. He brought his eyes back to where Marianne once stood and to his surprise, she was gone.

CHAPTER TWELVE
secret longing

Marianne stood upon the grand landing of Woodfeld Estate, a gilded world of charm and beauty unfolding below her. Through the ornate balustrades, she glimpsed the vibrant tableau—a sea of swirling gowns and tailored coats, vibrant discussions filling the air like effervescent bubbles. Light danced from a chandelier overhead, illuminating the joyful faces that hung on every word exchanged, especially around the centerpiece of the evening: Lady Emily Percy.

As each laugh echoed upward, Marianne felt the stirrings of longing tug at her heart, a bittersweet agony that intertwined the joy of being part of this splendid gathering with a profound sense of isolation. She shifted, her plain maid's attire a stark contrast to the gleaming dresses of the ladies below, who were aglow with admiration and envy shared for the sparkling announcement they were so eager to witness.

"Lord Grey's engagement to Lady Emily is quite the gossip. How delighted you must be for your employer, Miss Connelly," one maid remarked, leaning over the banister, a dreamy expression gracing her features.

A swell of voices followed, discussing the engagement as if it were an ethereal love story written by the hands of fate. But Marianne's heart twisted painfully at the sight of Lady Emily standing like a regal flower at the center of it all, her golden curls cascading elegantly over her shoulders, the very picture of a content bride-to-be. While the world saw the enchanting lady, Marianne held the parts that were unseen—the real Emily, who yearned for adventure wrapped in the fears of her impending commitments.

She glanced toward Lord Grey, who stood among the guests, his tall, athletic figure commanding yet relaxed, his expressive eyes shining like emeralds as they darted around the room. Even from a distance, Marianne felt the magnetic pull of his presence. How easy it would have been to step forward, to share even a fraction of her strength with him—to comfort him, to guide him as he navigated the sea of expectations that bound him. Yet she remained an observer in this exalted circle, caught in the whirlwind of emotions that swirled around her.

Marianne's reflection deepened as she overheard snippets of fervent conversation, punctuated by gasps of delight and speculative glances of admiration. The maids clustered nearby commented excitedly on the impending presentation of the engagement ring—a shimmering symbol of their union.

"Oh, it will be magnificent! Not one lady can rival Lady Emily's fortune!" another exclaimed, her tone practically dripping with admiration.

Marianne gritted her teeth, fighting back tears as she soaked in every syllable of praise directed toward her friend. She should share in the joy, to revel in Emily's happiness, yet her heart ached at the thought of what that happiness might mean for herself. With perilous clarity, she recalled their shared moments—the stolen glances, the cautious words, the laughter that felt so easy when it was just them—touches in the carriage. But now, all of that felt suspended in glass, a gorgeous reflection that separated her from the reality below.

As Lady Emily took the stage, the moment drew near, and with it, the heartbeats of all in attendance quickened in synchrony. Suddenly quiet fell over the rooms as Lord Grey made his move, eyes gleaming with a mixture of devotion and amusement. Marianne's breath caught in her throat.

From the very heart of the gathering emerged an aura of enchantment, dancing around Lord Edward like an extension of his very essence. He extended a treasure-trove box, its polished surface gleaming, drawing everyone's gaze. Marianne held her breath, each second stretching interminably as anticipation swelled in the air.

With a flourish born of rehearsed elegance, Lord Grey knelt before Lady Emily, producing the most exquisite ring, a dazzling sapphire flanked by diamonds that glinted like stars in the sky. The collective gasp of the crowd filled the air—a perfect harmony of wonder and awe.

The room, crisp with anticipation, reverberated with murmurs, the genteel excitement palpable. It was as if the atmosphere itself expanded to accommodate the significance of the moment, and Marianne felt unease tangle itself with shards of envy. The ring glittered like the promise of dreams yet to be fulfilled, and she was left to watch the facade play itself out, a bittersweet role she could have never imagined.

"Beautiful!" someone exclaimed amidst the startled whispers, while another lady remarked, "A match made in heaven!"

For a heartbeat, Marianne's world narrowed to the sight of Lord Grey's adoring gaze fixed upon Lady Emily, a look that spoke of wonder and connection. In that moment, Marianne's heart wrenched painfully; she could see the raw emotion shimmering in Edward's eyes—not for her but for Lady Emily—and a sharp pang of unrequited love invaded her thoughts. She was destined to remain at the periphery, the third wheel in a tapestry woven with threads of affection she could never hope to possess.

The ring settled upon Lady Emily's delicate finger glittered under the gaze of assembled admirers, illuminating her radiant smile as the applause erupted, echoing off the walls and enveloping the room in sheer jubilation. Admirers swarmed around Emily, showering her with praises and excitement, while Marianne remained frozen, an unshakable weight bearing down upon her chest.

As the euphoric laughter and cheers reverberated throughout the estate, Marianne took a step back, overwhelmed by the intensity of it all, paralyzed by an emotional storm. The warmth radiating from her friend, the joy in the crowd, all seemed to fade into a backdrop of sorrow. All she could do was watch, the image crystallizing of the life she would never lead and the man she could never call her own.

With a sharp intake of breath, she turned and fled the scene, her feet instinctively leading her toward the garden downstairs. The air outside felt cool against her flushed cheeks, a stark contrast to the warmth now absent from her heart as the door swung shut behind her, cutting her off from the laughter and celebration echoing within.

Once outside, surrounded by the gentle rustle of leaves and the soft glow of moonlight, the tears cascaded silently down Marianne's cheeks. The fragrant blossoms seemed to murmur soft comforts, echoing whispers that urged her to release the sorrow she had bottled inside. She did not dare to allow even a hint of this heartbreak to spill into the delight of Lady Emily's engagement. No, she vowed to remain supportive, steadfast in the face of unyielding pain, even as the turmoil corroded her insides.

With a heavy heart, Marianne pressed a hand against the cool stone of the garden wall, the night sky stretching above her like an unattainable dream. The stars twinkled brightly, indifferent. In that instance, she lost herself within her sorrows, allowing the heartbreak to flow freely—a silent cry beneath the absorbed beauty of the festivities still shimmering behind the confines of the estate.

THE SUN HUNG low in the sky as Marianne fled to the garden, the vibrant colors of the estate fading into a blur of greens and browns through her tear-filled eyes. The tall grasses swayed gently in the soft evening breeze, the rustling providing a calming backdrop to her distress. The air was thick with the scent of blooming flowers, a stark contrast to the ache that tightened around her heart.

Each step she took felt heavier than the last, her emotions weighing her down as she sprinted deeper into the forest. Ancient trees, their thick trunks gnarled with age, seemed to loom over her, their leaves whispering secrets. Marianne found refuge beneath one such tree, its bark cool against her back as she slid down to the ground. She drew her knees up to her chest and rested her forehead against them, allowing the sobs to escape her lips, the tears flowing freely as if they sought to cleanse her very soul.

Why must it hurt so much? she thought, a storm of feelings swirling within her. *Why did I let myself be swept away? I love him,* she concluded. *Why else would my heart ache so much?*

In the safety of her solitude, she tried to process all that had transpired. The kiss—the brief but electrifying connection they had shared—haunted her thoughts. It was a reckless decision, born of madness and adventure, she reminded herself, desperately clinging to reason. *What did I expect? For him to choose* **me** *over the safety of society?*

As she brushed the tears from her cheeks, a noise drew her attention—a crack of twigs and a rustle of leaves. Startled, she looked up to find Lord Grey standing there, just beyond the reach of her hiding place. He maintained a respectful distance, yet the way he stood so attentively, as if ready to rush forward yet hesitant to invade her space, sent her heart racing with a mix of panic and longing.

"Marianne," he began, his voice a low murmur that sent shivers down her spine. The vulnerability in his tone was palpable, echoing the turmoil she felt within. "I... I cannot get you out of my thoughts." He inhaled deeply, as if to fortify himself. "Our kiss... the carriage... they haunt me at night."

A part of her wanted to reach out, to acknowledge the truth of his words, but she felt a greater force holding her back—the unyielding grip of her reality, her livelihood. It is all she had. "What do you want from me, Lord Grey?" she asked, the words tasting bitter as they left her lips. "You have other obligations, my lord. You cannot be tied to a mere lady's maid."

Lord Grey's expression softened as he gazed upon Marianne, her tear-stained cheeks glistening in the fading light. He took a tentative step forward, his hand reaching out before falling back to his side. The air between them crackled with unspoken emotions, thick with the weight of their shared memories.

"Marianne," he began, his voice barely above a whisper, "I... I don't know how to express these foreign feelings. I only know that when I'm near you, everything else fades away." He ran a hand through his tousled hair, frustration evident in the gesture. "I am haunted by our night together, the laughter we shared, the connection we forged."

Marianne stood, brushing off her skirts as she tried to steady herself. Her heart raced, torn between the desire to rush into his arms and the need to maintain her composure. "My lord," she said, her voice trembling slightly, "we must not speak of such things. You are to be married to Lady Emily. It's... it's not proper."

Edward took another step closer, his eyes searching hers. "Proper? What of the feelings between us? Are we to ignore them for the sake of propriety?"

"We must," Marianne replied, her voice gaining strength even as her heart rebelled against her words. "Your duty lies with Lady Emily now. And mine... mine is to serve her faithfully." She turned away, unable to bear the intensity of his gaze.

Edward reduced the space between them, desperately holding back from wanting to seize her. "Marianne, are you interested in being my—"

"I will **not** be your mistress," she affirmed, finishing his sentence.

He hesitated, stunned by her admission, and the way his shoulders slumped felt like a physical blow. Edward's expression shifted, hurt flickering behind his deep green eyes. "And this is your reply?" he asked, voice tinged with disbelief.

No! Marianne thought, *How could I say such a thing?* with anguish raining down on her—she saw the light dim in his gaze, yet she pressed on, desperate to protect them both. "You have your future, and I have mine," she added, trying to fortify her resolve.

His hand reached out, capturing hers gently yet firmly, grounding her in the moment. "You're lying," he whispered, the disappointment dripping from his words like poison.

In his eyes, she could see he was searching for truths, desperately trying to unravel the tension between them. But the truth was too complicated, too dangerous.

Edward pulled his hand away, suddenly distant, holding back the words he could not speak. "I'll leave you to your thoughts," he declared, stepping back with a finality that sent her heart crashing against her ribs.

She watched him turn away, a sense of despair washing over her like an incoming tide.

As Edward walked away, his own internal turmoil battled within. *What do I truly want?* he pondered, struggling with the weight of expectations stacked against him. *Society's approval, the lure of a noble match... or the chance to forge my own path with a woman who makes me feel alive?*

But the choices came at a steep price, and he felt trapped, burdened by the knowledge that he was supposed to marry Lady Emily to fulfill responsibilities and expectations. Yet his heart yearned for the freedom he found with Marianne—the laughter, the adventure, the unexpected bond that had blossomed through the chaos.

As the distance between them widened, he couldn't shake the image of her—the lady's maid who had captured his heart in a whirlwind of adventure and mischief, a connection that lingered in the corners of his mind like an unfinished symphony.

Marianne remained beneath the ancient tree, the cool earth breathing in sync with her frantically beating heart. The cries of birds overhead, once joyful, now grating against her frayed nerves. She resolved not to cry anymore, yet the tears continued to fall, one after another. Each one felt like a wave crashing against the shore of her resolve.

A soft breeze stirred the air, carrying with it snippets of laughter from the party—unfettered joy that seemed so distant from her own heart. She clenched her fists, frustration bubbling up like a stubborn fountain.

Out of the corner of her eye, she spotted a flash of movement. "Maybe I can just run away," she murmured to the whispering leaves, a wild thought latching onto her mind like a reckless dream. But the notion was foolish; running away wouldn't solve anything. She was tethered to the life she had forged, one of loyalty and dutiful service.

But on second thought, subtracting herself from further pain did seem more appealing, and Marianne found her mind racing with possibilities. As she stood there, the cool night air caressing her flushed cheeks, a daring plan began to take shape in her mind. It was reckless, perhaps even foolish, but the allure of escape, of removing herself once and for all from this tangled web of emotions and expectations, was too strong to ignore. Her heart pounded with a mixture of fear and excitement as she contemplated the audacious steps she would need to take to free herself from this torment.

CHAPTER THIRTEEN
confessions

Morning sunlight streamed through the delicate lace curtains of Lady Emily's lavish room, casting playful shadows that danced across the opulent furnishings. The scent of fresh blooms wafted in from the garden, filling the air with a sweetness that felt almost mocking against the turmoil swirling within Marianne's heart. She busied herself straightening the embroidered cushions and tidying the elegant vanity, yet her thoughts were far from the routine tasks of a lady's maid.

As she arranged the beautifully folded silks, tension coursed through her. Every brush of fabric felt like a reminder of the twisted emotions entangled in her mind. Edward—Lord Grey—gathered in her thoughts like a storm, intimidating yet intoxicating. The exhilarating rush of their unexpected kiss haunted her, replacing the once-familiar rhythm of her heart with confusion and longing. No, she couldn't continue on this path. The weight of her feelings for him pushed her closer to the precipice of a decision she no longer could delay.

Taking in the serene beauty of the room, its elegance now seemed suffocating. Marianne finally steeled herself, her fingers trembling slightly as she reached for a feather duster to distract herself, all the while knowing it wouldn't do. She had come to a crossroads, and the only way forward rested upon the conviction she must find to deliver her resignation to Lady Emily.

Shifting her weight from one foot to the other, Marianne inhaled sharply. Her heart raced in anticipation of the confrontation ahead, yet with every beat, an ache tightened around her chest. She glanced toward the gilded mirror, catching her reflection—a woman torn between loyalty and love. Today was not merely another morning, but a day of reckoning.

With a determined breath, Marianne summoned her trusty courage and faced the door. Time to face the music, she thought, exiting the sanctuary of the chamber and stepping into the adjoining sitting room.

"Lady Emily," she began, the weight of her words churning in her stomach. Clutching the back of a plush armchair, she squared her shoulders. "May I have a word?"

Emily looked up from her journal, a serene smile blooming on her face, which immediately faltered as she studied Marianne's solemn expression.

"What is it?" Lady Emily asked with a hint of trepidation, sensing the gravity in Marianne's tone.

"I intend to resign," Marianne declared, her voice unwavering even as she felt the tremor in her resolve. "I cannot remain in your service."

A thick silence enveloped the room as Lady Emily's brow furrowed in confusion. Her surprise was evident, the color draining from her cheeks as she processed this unexpected proclamation. "Resign? But why?" she stammered, her bewilderment evident. "You've always been so devoted. I don't understand."

Tears pricked the corners of Marianne's eyes, and she swallowed hard, heart pounding in her chest. "It's complicated, Lady Emily... there are things—feelings—that I can no longer ignore," she managed, her breath hitching.

Lady Emily pushed herself off the chair, moving closer, her expression tinged with concern. "But you're not thinking clearly! Why would you even consider leaving? I value you far too much for that." The warmth in her voice felt like a salve yet pricked Marianne's heart all over again.

"I cannot stay," she repeated softly, clenching her fists at her sides. "With all that's happened... it would be best for my sake."

"Best for *your* sake?" Lady Emily's disbelief morphed into alarm. "Marianne, please, I dread losing you. I would never dismiss you, even after I'm married. You are more than a maid to me. You're family."

Marianne's heart fluttered, love and loyalty clashing within her. "Lady Emily," she whispered, "I would never have wanted you to feel burdened by my choice to leave. I simply cannot stand by and watch you embark on this—on your future with him."

"Who?" Lady Emily asked, confusion deepening in her features. "Is *he* the reason behind this?"

Silence stretched taut, hanging heavy between them. Every hesitation bore down against Marianne's chest, intensifying the turmoil inside. She thought her heart would burst as she battled with the impulse to either confess fully or hide in safety behind her loyalty to Emily.

After a moment, she found her voice, trembling but resolute. "I'm in love with Lord Grey," she confessed, the admission bursting forth, raw and unadorned.

Lady Emily's face froze, her expression shifting from worry to disbelief, her shock palpable, suffocating the atmosphere. The weight of Marianne's words hung in the air, enveloping them both in an uncomfortable stillness.

"What?" Lady Emily's response was softer than a whisper, eyes wide as she processed the statement. "You—what?"

Marianne braced herself against the ache in her heart, taking a step closer, yet the room felt like a cage. "I never meant for it to happen, but his kindness, his laughter… it makes my heart—"

Suddenly, the vulnerable exchange shifted within Lady Emily. The shock transformed into a rush of color that swept across her cheeks. Her eyes narrowed, and the atmosphere thickened with tension. "You cannot be serious," she snapped, her voice rising. "How could you, of all people, set your sights on him?"

"Lady Emily—I knew you would be hurt," Marianne pleaded, trying to keep her tone steady, though cracks ran deep in her resolve. "I respect you, that's why I've kept silent. But I cannot keep living this lie, nor can I ignore it anymore."

In a flurry of emotions, the green-eyed monster of jealousy unveiled itself in Lady Emily's demeanor. "A lie? What have I done to make you think that you could even consider pursuing Lord Grey? Were you two so intimate? Tell me now!"

Stung by the accusatory tone, Marianne straightened her back, head high despite the aching pain within her. "We shared a moment, a kiss—nothing more! But I have no inclination to pursue anything further, not against you," she stated, holding her ground. "But it isn't fair to let you believe I remain unaffected. I hadn't even wanted to confront my feelings. I wanted only to ensure your happiness!"

"Ensure *my* happiness," Emily echoed, incredulous. "By trying to steal my fiancé?" Lady Emily's hand moved before Marianne could react.

In a flash that felt suspended in time, Lady Emily struck Marianne's face, the sharp clap of skin against skin echoing in the suddenly silent room.

Stunned, Marianne stumbled back, shock and disbelief mingling in her chest. Never had she imagined such a betrayal from her dear friend.

"How dare you!" Emily exclaimed, her voice high and angry, filled to the brim with accusation. "You must have used your intimate closeness with him to worm your way into his affections! After all I've done for you, how can you turn on me like this?"

"Lady Emily, *please*," Marianne said softly, holding her cheek as her heart shattered into a thousand pieces. "You don't understand. I would never act so dishonorably. My love for him is but a burden I carry."

The silence enveloped them once more, a heavy pall hanging between friends turned adversaries. Lady Emily stood there, breathing heavily, the realization of the rift scorched into the air between them. The bond, once strong and steadfast, lay frail before them, fraying under the strain of raw emotions and confessions that had erupted beyond their control.

"Go from my sight," Lady Emily seethed, "You *disgust* me."

THE ECHO of the slap hung in the air, a harsh punctuation to their conversation. Marianne touched her cheek, the tingling sensation radiating outward—a stinging reminder of the rift that had shattered their years of friendship. Stunned into silence, she could barely breathe as the weight of Lady Emily's fury settled heavily around her, transforming the once-picturesque room into a suffocating cage.

Inside, her heart twisted like a taut string under pressure, her thoughts a chaotic storm crashing against the rocks of resolve. Was this how their bond would end, severed by an impulsive act of rage? She had always been loyal, always supportive, yet in this moment, with the pain of the slap still vivid against her skin, she understood that loyalty alone could not mend the fractures between them.

The silence deepened, stretching onward until it felt eternal. Lord Grey's name hung unspoken but heavy in the air, a ghost that loomed larger than life, festering until even the shadows felt uncomfortable. More than the physical pain, it was the affront to their connection that carved a deeper wound. A decision solidified within her—a fierce resolution to reclaim her identity beyond the walls of Woodfeld Estate.

As she turned from the confrontation with Lady Emily, memories flooded her mind like a river, their currents carrying her away from the present. The hum of life within the estate faded, leaving her in an almost dreamlike state as she resolved to pack away her few personal belongings. She had always cherished the moments with Emily, and now she would have to pack those memories as well.

She moved methodically, her fingers brushing against the delicate fabrics of her uniforms—each touch flooding her with nostalgia. The soft cotton felt cool against her skin, eliciting visions of shared laughter and late-night conversations that now felt like ephemeral dreams. Each dress, each cloak transported her back to the times they roamed the gardens, plotting flights of fancy and watching the world feel more alive than it ever had.

A small vial of potpourri caught her attention next—lady's slippers and lavender, the delightful aroma that once wafted through the pathways of their shared space. Now, it felt achingly bittersweet, as if it held the spirits of their friendship trapped within. She inhaled deeply, savoring the scent one last time, as a fresh pang of grief punctuated her heart.

Handling her few treasured items made the weight of her decision unbearable yet somehow liberating. Each piece she folded into her satchel had been witness to their camaraderie: the silk ribbons, the letters of encouragement, the tiny keepsakes from their shared escapades. Yet knowing she would be leaving them behind filled her with a unique sense of power. There was a girl in this room—once a lady's maid—who longed for more than the duty her title prescribed. This new Marianne yearned to venture into the unpredictable tides of life, embracing uncertainty as a companion.

With the last of her few belongings tucked away, she stole one final glance around the room, her heart heavy yet buoyed by resolve. She navigated the familiar corridors of Woodfeld Estate one last time, her footsteps remarkably steady despite the flurry of emotions brewing inside her. The opulence that surrounded her, once a comforting embrace, now felt like golden chains shackling her to a past she was determined to escape.

And as she stepped through the grand doors of Woodfeld Estate, it felt as if she were tangibly leaving a piece of her heart behind. The grandiosity of the estate faded into the distance, the thrumming echoes of upset and love left trapped within the gilded halls. With each step away from the only home she had ever known, she felt the strain of the past unravel, giving way to the budding hope that lay on the horizon.

As she crossed the threshold of what had been her life, a swell of liberation surged through her—each step forward imbued with newfound strength. The carved path stretched ahead, lined with the strong oaks that whispered around her. Uncertainty clawed at her thoughts, but it was accompanied by the promise of possibilities yet to come.

Before she turned a final corner, Marianne hesitated, stealing one last look at the estate bathed in the warm light of the setting sun, an image of both beauty and confinement. Her heart felt heavy, and a lump formed in her throat as bittersweet reminiscence flooded her mind.

Yet in that moment, Marianne turned forward, embracing the unknown ahead. The path that loomed before her whispered with the potential of adventures yet unbidden, an entirely new chapter waiting to be written. Embracing her fate, she stepped from the shadow of Woodfeld Estate and into the embrace of her own liberation, a world alive with endless uncertainty—each breath pregnant with promise.

CHAPTER FOURTEEN
departure from london

A soft glow crept into the early morning sky, filtering through the haze of London's streets and illuminating the bustling coach station. The air held a crisp freshness, a promise of the day that beckoned with new possibilities. Marianne stood amidst the chaos, a small bag of belongings clutched tightly in her hand, her heart racing as she observed the flurry of activity surrounding her. Horse-drawn carriages rattled on cobblestone streets as the calls of drivers mingled with the wakeful sounds of vendors setting up their stalls, all marking the commencement of another busy day in the sprawling city.

To an outsider, it was a scene of charming disorder. However, for Marianne, it represented a turning point, a gateway to a life distinctly different from the one she had known as Lady Emily's maid. Even as she admired the kaleidoscope of life whirling around her, a bittersweet pang tugged at her heart, joining the chorus of excitement thrumming through her veins. *This is it*, she thought, her breath hitching as she absorbed the essence of her former world one last time.

Pressing through the throng, she approached the weathered ticket booth, her pulse quickening at every small jingle of coins in her pocket. Each step felt heavier than the last, as if a tangible force was pulling her back into her old life, back into London's suffocating embrace. *Am I really ready for this?* The doubts swirled as vividly as the light spilling over the station. Each face she passed mirrored a life that might have been hers, a reminder of the comfort she was leaving behind.

Taking a deep breath, Marianne stepped up to the window, her expression determined yet fragile. The ticket seller regarded her with a mixture of indifference and mild annoyance, awaiting her request. "One ticket to Yorkshire, please," she managed, her voice a steady tremor amid the bustling noise around them.

The man turned away, showcasing a wall adorned with destinations, a map of possibilities. As the inked letters caught her eye, her heart sank further at the thought of emptying her hard-earned savings. Yet, mingling with the trepidation was an undeniable thrill, a flicker of freedom warming her chest. *Independence...* the word echoed like a sweet refrain in her mind.

"Five shillings," he declared, startling her from her reverie. And so, she fished the currency from her pocket; the metallic clinks resonated in a mocking melody against the heavy silence of her thoughts. Her fingers brushed against familiar coins, each one representing her sacrifice, her longing for a life unshackled by the expectations of society.

With a heart still grappling with uncertainty, Marianne handed over her hard-won money. In exchange, the ticket seller offered a flimsy piece of parchment, its edges worn yet brimming with the promise of relocation: a ticket to a future she was desperate to claim.

Marianne stepped away from the booth, feeling the weight of her decision solidifying as she unfolded the ticket, examining the printed letters that spelled out **YORKSHIRE**—one word, yet it transported her thoughts to an expansive landscape of rolling hills and open skies, inviting her to shed the skin of the past.

As the bustle of the station enveloped her, she took a moment to reflect. London was not merely a backdrop of brick and mortar; it was her decidedly genteel prison. Here, she had forged laughter and joy with Lady Emily, but those feelings coexisted with strain and expectation. A mixture of guilt and resolve tightened around her heart, reminding her of the emotional bond they had shared. Yet, she resolved to remember only the bright moments—the whispered secrets, the shared hopes, the adventures seeking to overwhelm everything around them. And, thank goodness, she was not with child! A bastard child would only complicate things beyond measure, throwing her carefully laid plans into utter disarray. Marianne felt a profound sense of relief wash over her when she started her monthly flow, the tension that had been coiled tightly in her chest finally unwinding. She allowed herself a moment to breathe deeply, savoring the knowledge that at least this particular worry could be set aside. The consequences of her actions, while still daunting, now seemed slightly more manageable without the added burden of an unexpected pregnancy looming over her head.

Letting out a sigh, she committed to a mental farewell, murmuring silent goodbyes to Lady Emily Percy—*may her happiness find its way in the company of Lord Grey, and may mischief abound in her future*. Engulfed by the sights and sounds—a last echo of carriages rattling, the heady scent of freshly baked bread wafting through the air—Marianne glanced back one final time toward the chaos. Every element served as a reminder of the life she was leaving behind, a past ripe with tangled relationships and societal expectations.

Navigating through the crowd, she climbed aboard the coach, her heart fluttering with excitement and trepidation. Settling into the worn leather seat, she allowed her mind to wander through thoughts of the life awaiting her in Yorkshire. *I shall find work, something simple yet fulfilling,* she planned, envisioning herself serving in a quaint inn, interacting with the patrons who came and went, sharing tales of their lives. There was a certain exhilaration in imagining new beginnings. Yet, the memories lingered like echoes of her past, hinting at the societal biases that would follow her as the shadow of a lady's maid.

The coach jolted slightly as it set off, the distant sounds of London fading into the pull of the countryside. The warm sun streamed through the window, capturing Marianne's pensive expression as thoughts danced back to the realities of her situation. With every mile, she would be shedding pieces of herself, reveling in the opportunity of independence while simultaneously grappling with the uncertainty of her identity outside of Woodfeld Estate.

What could "Marianne Connelly" become away from the nurturing arms of Woodfeld? Marianne crushed her hands into her lap, absorbing the growing landscape rolling past the window —fields of bright blooms, glowing golden under the sun's embrace. Every mile felt like a shifting of fate, an awakening stirring within her spirit.

Her mind danced with possibilities as the coach rattled along. She imagined herself strolling through quiet villages, filled with lively innkeepers who could provide her with a fresh start—a vibrant contrast to the predictable landscapes of her former life. The thought alone began to breathe life into her weary soul.

Yet anxiety crept back in like the chilling winds of uncertainty. As the stops began at several quaint inns, each was bustling with patrons, laughter mingling with the clinking of glassware—

marrying joy with laughter. Marianne, at each destination, felt her nerves bubble to the surface like an uninvited guest. She watched intently as lively conversations surrounded her, her heart pounding against her ribs. Stepping down from the coach, she gathered the last shreds of her courage, adjusting her attire as she prepared to enter the first inn.

"Good morning!" she called out brightly, catching the attention of the innkeeper. "I'm seeking a position, if you have any vacancies."

The brief smile on the innkeeper's face faded against the awkward laughter that followed, with patrons glancing away or rolling their eyes dismissively. After polite conversation dripping with false pleasantries, he gently turned her down, pointing towards another place that might have opportunities.

Thus began the cycle—upbeat inquiries, soft-spoken rejections. Each time she stepped back onto the street, Marianne felt a slight sting of humiliation wash over her, the lively atmosphere contrasting sharply with the ache of rejection. While the patrons appeared to be full of merry, she could not shake the shadows wrapping tightly around her budding hopes. *Is this what a new beginning feels like?*

With each failed inquiry, Marianne felt the threads of courage fray, her resolve starting to wear thin. Yet, within her, flickered the flame of determination. She would not let the door close behind her without a fight; the sweet taste of independence beckoned like a siren song. Ignoring the heaviness, she lifted her chin with renewed vigor, stepping toward the next inn with resolve suffused with hope.

THE INN GREETED Marianne like an old friend, its cozy atmosphere enveloping her with warmth that she had longed for since leaving Woodfeld Estate. She stepped through the door, trailing in a gust of fresh air that wafted in from outside. A crackling fire danced in the stone hearth, casting flickering shadows through the inviting space. The faint aroma of roasted chestnuts intermingled with the scent of woodsmoke, and she felt a pang of comfort sweep through her, reminding her of softer moments.

She made her way to a sturdy oak table near the fire, where a gentle smile awaited her from the gentleman seated across it. He sported a tousled mop of dark curls and twinkling blue eyes, exuding an amiable aura that immediately put her at ease. Perhaps he had noticed the weariness etched upon her face as she joined him, and he gestured to the empty seat across from him.

"Welcome, my lady. You look like you could use a warm drink and some friendly company," he said, lifting a mug that steered sweet scents into the air. "Might I interest you in a cup of hot chocolate? It's made with our finest cocoa."

Marianne, her heart buoyed by the gentleman's radiant kindness, accepted the offer with a nod. "That would be lovely, thank you." Her voice came out softer than usual, but the warmth of the inn coaxed out her confidence.

As they waited for the steaming concoction, the gentleman eyed her curiously. "You seem new to these parts. What brings you to our cozy little haven?"

Marianne hesitated. The road to Yorkshire had been fraught with uncertainties, but this simple conversation felt like a reprieve from her relentless thoughts. "I'm seeking work. My position as a lady's maid has come to an end, and I was hoping to find another opportunity."

"Oh, indeed?" His brows lifted slightly, and that charming smile broadened. "You might be in luck then. I happen to know that Mrs. Dover, a fine lady with a good heart, is searching for a new lady's maid following the recent departure of her last one. Quite the scandal it has caused among the locals, really."

Marianne's heart raced as his words sunk in. Mrs. Dover! The name rang like a melodious chime in her ears. With the prospect of employment dancing into view, her spirits soared as she envisioned herself stepping into a life of independence once more. She leaned forward, urgency threading her voice. "Do you think she would consider me for the position? I've worked diligently for my last mistress, and I possess the skills needed to serve her well."

The gentleman chuckled softly. "She might very well appreciate your enthusiasm! The family's upcoming soirée requires ample preparation—there's quite the flurry of activity surrounding it. I imagine she would need a reliable pair of hands by her side."

"Could you tell me how I might go about contacting Mrs. Dover?" Marianne asked, eager anticipation bubbling in her chest.

"Of course!" He produced a scrap of parchment from his coat pocket, scribbling notes to share Mrs. Dover's residence and a few choice remarks about the lady's character. "Here you are. Do not hesitate to introduce yourself; I believe she will welcome your application with open arms."

Marianne accepted the parchment with trembling fingers, gratitude spilling from her. "Thank you, sir. I appreciate your kindness more than words can express."

"Not at all! We all deserve a bit of good fortune now and again," he said, beaming.

As she took her leave of the inn, the bright sunlight of the day cast a golden glow around her, invigorating her spirit for the journey ahead. Each step toward the waiting carriage filled her with excitement, and yet an undercurrent of anxiety settled within her. Not only was she leaving London behind, along with the tangled threads of her past, but she was boldly stepping into the unknown.

Her thoughts swirled with reflection as she sat within the confines of the carriage, the cushioned seat feeling plush beneath her. She considered her time with Lady Emily and Lord Grey, the rollercoaster of emotions that had consumed her days and nights. The weight of their expectations had dulled her spirit; their enchanting world had woven a fabric that suffocated her longing for something real, something of her own.

Marianne's mind drifted to the impending marriage that loomed on the horizon, a union that seemed to come with a sense of inevitability. She imagined Lady Emily, ever the spirited whirlwind, would seize upon the urgency of the situation, hastening the plans with her characteristic enthusiasm. The thought made Marianne's heart ache a little; she felt a wave of sympathy for Lord Grey, the charming rake whose presence had ignited emotions within her that she had never fully acknowledged. The absence of his teasing banter and smoldering gaze left a palpable void in her days, and she realized just how deeply she missed him.

Now, as the carriage bumped along the uneven roads towards Mrs. Dover's estate, Marianne felt the gentle twinge of determination knitting its way through her heart. "I refuse to be tethered by their choices any longer," she whispered to herself, basking in the freedom that bloomed.

The landscape outside the carriage window morphed from the bustling backdrop of London into the undulating greenery of the countryside, each rolling hill a promise of fresh beginnings. Birds flitted between branches, their melodious songs lifting her spirits higher as if resounding her own desires. A sense of possibility washed over her, and the fears that had clung stubbornly to her thoughts began to dissipate like morning mist beneath the sun.

She conjured dreams of her new life with Mrs. Dover, envisioning her fulfilling her duties with grace and competence. Perhaps this new position would grant her the chance to cultivate her independence, to become the lady's maid she had always aspired to be rather than simply an afterthought in someone else's story. She imagined herself busy with the tasks of preparing for the evening gatherings that awaited—a confident figure focused on her ambitions rather than bound to the specters of her past.

Yet with each joyous thought came a whisper of doubt. What if she failed to impress? What if Mrs. Dover deemed her unsuitable? The weight of vulnerability lingered, but Marianne chose to embrace it rather than shy away. With resolve inching its way into her heart, she wrestled with the question of her future—what might it behold?

As the carriage finally neared its destination, the expansive grounds of Mrs. Dover's estate sprang into view, adorned with an array of blooming flowers and manicured hedges. Each vibrant color spoke of splendid gatherings and bustling life within those walls. It reminded her that opportunity awaited within the confines, waiting to embrace her as she took one tentative step forward.

"Today begins a new chapter," she whispered, her heart pounding against her ribs.

With that thought pulsing through her, she gazed out of the carriage window, entranced by the magnificent landscape. A dawning sense of hope illuminated her features, illuminating the path that lay ahead.

As the carriage rolled to a halt, Marianne prepared to step from her past and into a realm of uncertainty laced with promise, the thrill and trepidation of what lay beyond calling her ever closer.

epilogue

YORKSHIRE - SIX MONTHS LATER

In the heart of Yorkshire, the sun poured golden light over the undulating hills, painting a scene that felt almost idyllic in its tranquility. Wildflowers danced amid the gentle breeze, their vibrant hues adding splashes of color to the lush green landscape. This was a far cry from the frenetic pulse of London, a world away from societal obligations and whispered gossip. Here, Marianne found herself embracing a life that felt both familiar and profoundly new.

As she moved through the spacious, light-filled rooms of Dover House, the sound of laughter and chatter filled the air. Her heart swelled with contentment as she attended to the needs of Mrs. Dover, her charming employer. The widow had welcomed Marianne into her home with open arms, offering her not merely a position but a friendship that flourished amidst their shared moments.

In the solitude of Mrs. Dover's dressing room, sunbeams filtered through lace curtains, illuminating the elegance of the vintage furnishings. Marianne stood behind the seated Mrs. Dover, her deft fingers weaving the silken strands of the older woman's hair into a delicate updo, elegant and poised.

"Do be careful with that comb, my dear," Mrs. Dover teased, a twinkle in her eye. "One too many tugs, and I may end up looking like a frightful hedgehog."

"Oh, Mrs. Dover," Marianne replied with an airy laugh, her heart warmed by their camaraderie. "You'll always be a dazzling beauty, regardless of any mishaps I might cause—though I shall take great care not to make you resemble one of those prickly creatures."

The room filled with bright laughter, an intimate moment shared between the two that highlighted the bond they had cultivated. Mrs. Dover's eyes sparkled as she studied Marianne in the mirror, proud of the vibrant young woman who had grown from the timid lady's maid needing direction to an independent spirit who not only radiated confidence but also made a genuine impact in her life.

With light chatter, Mrs. Dover's voice shifted, tinged with a hint of excitement. "Speaking of dazzling affairs, we're hosting a dinner party next week. I expect it to be rather momentous."

Marianne's heart leaped at the prospect. "Oh, how splendid! Who will be our guests?"

Mrs. Dover turned, a knowing smile playing on her lips. "Everyone's favorite nobility, of course. I've invited several titled guests—though I suspect you will have your work cut out for you."

The conversation shifted subtly as Mrs. Dover continued arranging her hair, moving seamlessly from lighthearted banter about the evening's plans to discussing seasonal changes that brought forth the singular beauty of Yorkshire's countryside. It gave Marianne the luxury of time to turn the prospect of the dinner in her mind, her heart racing at the prospect of seeing familiar faces within the tapestry of guests.

After a few moments filled with gentle laughter, Mrs. Dover added with a twinkle in her eye, "I do believe your delightful skills will be put to good use. It bodes well for your future, you know? Managing the likes of titled gentry? I dare say it may even lead to... some irreducible magic."

Marianne did not fully grasp the weight of Mrs. Dover's words, her focus twirling like the sun-drenched leaves outside. Meeting so many titled guests after being ensconced within the estate for months both excited and terrified her. Each new role and identity seemed intertwined with past choices, yet reaffirmed that she was no longer a mere lady's maid without ambition.

As Marianne prepared to step back into the busier world of guests, the day unfolded like a bright lotus blooming in the afternoon sun. Activity swirled around her as various staff members gathered to plan for the upcoming dinner party; the excitement filled the house, a mix of quiet conversations blended with the fresh scent of flowers being arranged for the event.

All hands were on deck, creating a harmonious orchestration of movement within the household. Staff fluttered about, ensuring that every detail was recognized—tables laid with the finest china, fresh blooms adorning surfaces, and linens smoothed into perfection. Morris, the butler, barked orders, yet there lingered a sense of joy among the servants—a shared anticipation that made the day seem less daunting.

As Marianne joined her fellow staff members in the kitchen to assist with preparations, her heart brimmed with a newfound energy. She exchanged banter with the cook while chopping vegetables, a joyful routine marking the rhythm of their day.

The cook, Mrs. Hargrove, stood at the hearth, expertly stirring a pot filled with a fragrant concoction of meats and vegetables that promised to warm hearts on the brisk Yorkshire evening. Marianne couldn't help but marvel at the transformable magic that unfolded with every meal.

"Looking forward to the grand dinner, are you, Mrs. Hargrove?" Marianne asked, wiping her hands on her apron as she approached the stout figure of the cook.

Mrs. Hargrove paused her stirring and turned with a twinkle in her eye, flour-dusting her apron like a badge of honor. "Of course, love! Nothing gets me as excited as a gathering at Dover House. Fine company, good food, and the chance to show off my mastery at the stove—it's simply splendid!"

Marianne chuckled at the cook's enthusiasm. "I daresay you'll have plenty of oohs and aahs tonight. Your roast is the stuff of legends, including the pine nut stuffing. Why, I still dream of it sometimes!"

Mrs. Hargrove's flourish of a hand accompanied her laughter as she replied, "Flattery will get you everywhere, my dear! It's all practice and a dollop of love, you see? With a pinch of chaos in the kitchen thrown in for good measure. Now, what's on your mind as you help me prep?"

Marianne glanced around the kitchen, excitement bubbling within her, echoing that familiar thrill from her earlier time in London. "I was just thinking about the guests. Mrs. Dover did say we'll have nobles and their ilk, did she not?"

"Aye," Mrs. Hargrove responded, leaning slightly closer as if sharing a secret. "A veritable smattering of the ton, if I've heard correctly. Word around the kitchen is that some of those young lords are dreadfully keen on impressing the ladies—they're bound to strut their stuff tonight."

Marianne thought about her past in service to the Viscount and Viscountess of Woodfeld. She laughed, the image forming in her mind as Mrs. Hargrove continued chopping fresh carrots into precise rounds. "You mean they're going to parade about, showing off their finery like peacocks?"

"Precisely! Just wait until they start in on their stories of bravado—how they jousted in the moonlight or dined with dukes. Oho, it's a sight to be seen!" Mrs. Hargrove leaned back against the counter, her hands never missing a beat even as they shared in delightful imaginings.

"Who knows, Mrs. Hargrove?" Marianne offered, a teasing lilt to her voice as she continued with the preparation. "Perhaps I will steal the spotlight from those dashing lords completely!"

"Oh, but methinks you already have the talent and charm to ensnare any unguarded heart in the room!" the cook replied, her laugh melding with the playful air of camaraderie surrounding them.

And as the afternoon sun continued to blaze outside the tall windows, Marianne felt a thrill course through her spirit. The dinner might be filled with lords and ladies, but tonight she would be part of something special, willingly weaving herself into the fabric of relationships and connections that transcended the mundane roles they held.

"Come now, dear," Mrs. Hargrove beckoned as she gave Marianne a knowing smile. "Back to our preparations. We've a sumptuous feast to create, and those nobles aren't going to dazzle themselves, are they?"

With renewed vigor, Marianne smiled brightly, her heart pounding with possibilities as she joined in harmony with the bustle of the kitchen—the laughter and the shared dreams floating through the air, merging into a delightful tapestry of hope and sincerity.

However, a sharper moment of clarity echoed through the bustling atmosphere when the butler called out to them. "Staff, we shall greet our guests outside! Everyone needs to take their position. Line up according to rank!" he added, drawing laughter as team members exchanged bemused glances.

Marianne took a deep breath at the thought of standing among the rest, yet her nerves fizzled in the excitement of seeing numerous notable faces again. In the midst of the stirring anticipation, she felt a bond with her fellow staff, their collective purpose linking them in a simple moment of joy.

She straightened her dress, smoothed out any creases, and fell into line, the heartwarming notion of belonging wrapped around her like a soft blanket. For all her thoughts of insecurities and humility in her role, she was where she wanted to be—no longer a shadow in the background, but a part of something greater, one hand in the service of a household rich in warmth, laughter, and community.

THE LATE AFTERNOON sun dipped below the horizon, casting a golden hue over the sprawling grounds of Dover House. Marianne stood at her post in the entrance, her heart racing in time with the rhythmic clattering of hooves on cobblestones as carriages began to arrive. She took a deep breath, absorbing the late-summer air filled with the scents of blooming roses and freshly cut grass.

As the first carriage pulled up, Marianne felt a flutter of excitement. The footman opened the door, and a distinguished gentleman stepped out, followed closely by a poised lady. Lord and Lady Huxley emerged with an air of grace that captivated those who watched.

"Welcome, my dears!" Mrs. Dover's voice rang out, warm and inviting as she approached the new guests, hands clasped together in a display of genuine delight. Lord Huxley doffed his hat courteously, while Lady Huxley, a vision of elegance in a flowing gown of emerald green, returned Mrs. Dover's greeting with dignified warmth.

Marianne, catching her breath at the sight of the lovely couple, yearned to impress them. She curtsied as Lady Huxley turned her gaze in Marianne's direction, the lady's eyes sparkling with kindness.

"This is my lady's maid, Miss Connelly," Mrs. Dover introduced, gesturing toward Marianne, who felt a swell of pride accompany the honor of being presented so formally.

"A pleasure, Miss Connelly," Lady Huxley said, the light of her smile radiating charm. "I do hope you are prepared for a most splendid evening."

"Of course, your ladyship," Marianne replied, barely containing her eagerness. "I shall be at your service throughout the evening."

The Huxleys exchanged a smile, and Marianne felt buoyed by the warmth of their approval. They were just the first of a long line of esteemed guests, and anticipation buzzed in her veins.

As the pleasant chatter resumed, another carriage arrived—a sleek, black vehicle accentuated with gilded embellishments. The footman alighted, opening the door to reveal Mrs. Fischer, a familiar figure who filled Mrs. Dover with nostalgia. The older woman's lively demeanor exuded a warmth that felt like a familiar embrace.

"Charlotte, dear!" Mrs. Fischer exclaimed, bustling toward her. "I'm so delighted to have seen your invitation. I haven't been to Dover House in years."

"Why, Mrs. Fischer! It is wonderful to see you again," Mrs. Dover gushed, stepping forward and enveloping her in a joyful hug. Their laughter harmonized with the gentle breeze, creating a vibrant atmosphere that filled the entrance hall.

Just as the conviviality settled into a comfortable rhythm, a final carriage rolled to a stop at the entrance—this time, with added drama to its arrival. The door swung open with an authoritative flair, revealing none other than—Lord Edward Grey. Every smattering of chatter dissipated as he stepped onto the steps, his tall stature exuding a charisma that made heads turn.

Marianne's breath stilled at the sight of him. His dark hair was tousled playfully, and he wore a tailored ensemble that accentuated the lines of his physique, all confidence and charm. There was an enthusiasm about him that enveloped the atmosphere; even the staff couldn't help but cast glances cloaked in admiration and curiosity.

Marianne's heart raced as Lord Grey approached Mrs. Dover, his easy smile and graceful movements captivating everyone present. She couldn't help but drink in the sight of him, noting how time had only enhanced his allure. His deep green eyes sparkled with warmth as he took Mrs. Dover's hand, bowing slightly in a gesture of respect and familiarity.

"My dear Mrs. Dover," Edward said, his rich voice carrying across the entrance hall. "How wonderful to see you again after all this time. You look as radiant as ever."

Mrs. Dover's face lit up with genuine pleasure. "Lord Grey, what a delight! I must say, you've grown into quite the gentleman since I last saw you."

Edward chuckled, a sound that sent a shiver down Marianne's spine. "You're too kind, madam. I hope I've improved somewhat since my days of childhood mischief in your gardens."

Mrs. Dover's eyes twinkled with nostalgia. "Ah, those were the days. I've missed your visits, Edward. The house hasn't been quite the same since my dear Henry passed. You used to bring such life and laughter when you came to see him."

A shadow of sadness passed over Edward's features, quickly replaced by a gentle smile. "Your husband was a remarkable man, Mrs. Dover. I learned a great deal from him, and I cherish the memories of our conversations in his study."

Marianne watched the exchange with fascination, her curiosity piqued by this glimpse into Lord Grey's past. She had known him only as the rakish nobleman of London society, but here he seemed different—more genuine, perhaps even vulnerable.

Mrs. Dover patted Edward's arm affectionately. "Well, my boy, you must tell me all about your adventures since we last met. I hear you've become quite the talk of London society."

Edward's smile turned slightly rueful. "Ah, yes. I'm afraid my reputation often precedes me these days. But I assure you, Mrs. Dover, I haven't forgotten the lessons of propriety you and your husband instilled in me." As he surveyed the scene, his gaze shifted, sweeping over the neatly arranged decorum then did a double-take on one member of the Dover household.

Marianne?

Time slowed as their eyes locked, an electric surge igniting the air between them.

Marianne felt warmth flood her cheeks, a familiar thrill cascading through her veins even as she contemplated their turbulent past. But what startled her was the way he seemed to relax; the tension melted from his shoulders as he approached her, a soft smile gracing his lips.

"Miss Connelly," he breathed, his voice smooth and filled with an unmistakable warmth that sent excitement bubbling within her. He stepped towards her locale.

"Lord Grey," she curtsied. "What a wonderful surprise to see you here," she blurted, even as her heart raced from the overwhelming emotions swelling within.

Marianne instinctively looked past him, half-expecting to see Lady Emily emerge from the shadows, but the absence of her friend filled her with an unsettling feeling. "And your wife?" she asked, surprised by the urgency in her own tone.

Mrs. Dover walked over to the twosome and suddenly interceded, "What's this? What is your acquaintance with my lady's maid? And, more importantly, what is this about a wife Lord Grey? When did you get married?"

Lord Grey swiftly distanced himself from Mrs. Dover and guided Miss Connelly away from the growing commotion. "Just a brief word with your attendant, Mrs. Dover, and I guarantee you'll be fully informed of the situation, you have my word," he assured her.

Lord Grey's composure faltered slightly. He glanced toward the crowd, lowering his voice to ensure the curiosity of nearby staff, Mrs. Dover and now Mrs. Fischer, kept at bay. "We did not marry," he confessed, the weight of those words lingering heavily in the air.

The disclosure hit Marianne like an abrupt breeze, making her pulse quicken with an unforeseen excitement. "Yet you presented her with a band. You openly asked for her hand in marriage."

Edward's confession hung in the air, heavy with the weight of unspoken emotions. He clutched his hat tightly in his hands, his fingers restlessly tracing the brim as if seeking comfort in the familiar texture. His usually confident demeanor had given way to a rare display of vulnerability, his shoulders slightly hunched as he stood before her.

"Yes," he repeated, his voice barely above a whisper. The word seemed to escape his lips with great effort, as though it carried the burden of a thousand unspoken truths. His piercing gaze locked onto hers, a tempest of earnestness and raw emotion swirling in their depths. The intensity of his stare was almost palpable, conveying a depth of feeling that words alone could not express.

"I could not marry her," Edward continued, his voice gaining strength even as it quavered with the enormity of his admission. He paused, drawing a shaky breath before plunging ahead. "Not when I have found myself in love with someone else."

The last words hung between them, charged with possibility and fraught with implications. In that moment, the world around them seemed to fade away, leaving only the electric connection of their shared gaze and the thunderous beating of their hearts.

"With whom?" Marianne asked, her heart beating a mile a minute, each thud echoing the thrill of anticipation that coursed through her veins. Her fingers unconsciously tightened around the fabric of her skirt, creasing the well-worn cotton as she leaned forward, eager for the answer. The air seemed to thicken with tension, and she found herself holding her breath, afraid that even the slightest movement might shatter this pivotal moment.

"With you, silly," Edward confessed, his fingers fidgeting with his hat once more, as if it could somehow ground him amidst the whirlwind of emotions swirling around them. His eyes, usually so confident and mischievous, now held a vulnerability that caught Marianne off guard. The air between them seemed to crackle with an electric tension, making every breath feel significant. Edward's gaze darted between Marianne's face and the ground, his usual composure slipping away to reveal a man teetering on the edge of something profound and terrifying.

The moment felt tense, exciting, and scary. Marianne's heart filled with unexpected happiness that almost overwhelmed her. Tears formed in her eyes as she tried to understand what he had said. "Me?" she whispered, afraid speaking too loudly might ruin the moment.

His gaze smoldered with ardor, the words tumbling forth in a husky confession, "The instant our eyes first met, you bewitched me utterly. Your vivacious essence breathes new life into my soul." He took a step closer, his presence electrifying. "I yearn to properly woo you, to embark upon this tantalizing journey and discover where the trail may lead us."

Marianne's heart soared, and she found herself nodding, a grin breaking through her stunned expression.

He extended his arm, inviting her forth. "Shall we take a turn of the garden?"

"Yes," she replied, her heart racing at the suggestion. "Yes, let's."

As they stepped alongside one another, weaving their way away from the bustling crowd, Marianne felt a delightful sense of excitement unfurl within her chest, like the petals of a flower greeting the dawn. This was a chance to forge something new, something vibrant and uncharted, together. The air around them seemed to shimmer with possibilities, and she could scarcely contain the thrill that made her heart race.

"Miss Connelly, may I ask you a question?" Lord Grey's voice was soft, almost hesitant.

Marianne's heart sank, a leaden weight settling in her stomach. And there it was—the dreaded question he'd asked twice before. She closed her eyes, steeling herself for disappointment. "Yes, my lord. You may."

"Are you open to courtship?" Lord Grey asked, his tone teasing yet filled with sincerity. His eyes, usually so guarded, now shone with an earnestness that took her breath away.

Marianne smiled, relishing in the moment while feigning reluctance. She bit her lower lip, pretending to contemplate her answer. "Yes, I suppose I am."

"Last question," he said plainly, his gaze never leaving her face.

Marianne turned her head slightly, bracing for the pain she was certain would follow. Her fingers twisted nervously in the folds of her dress, her breath catching in her throat. She missed him so deeply that she would say yes to anything.

Edward reached for her, sweeping her into his arms as if to cage the air around them. The warmth of his embrace sent a shiver down her spine, and she found herself lost in the depths of his eyes. He leaned in a fraction closer, his breath ghosting across her cheek before uttering, "Will you accept my hand in marriage, my dearest Marianne?"

THE END

you might also like...

the surprise heir
BY TRISHA FUENTES

In the charming era of Regency England, a tale of unexpected love and enduring destinies unfolds. **Edmund Gallagher**, a distant relative to the prestigious Lord of Langston Hall, lives a modest life far removed from the grandeur of his noble kin. His childhood memories of Langston Hall are few, but one delightful memory of climbing a treehouse with the young lord, **Rupert Hargrove**, continues to warm his heart through the years.

Now, decades later, Rupert, hailed as the dashing heir to Langston Hall, is poised to marry the impeccable Miss Abigail Stronghold, securing his personal happiness and a prosperous future for the estate. However, just as wedding bells are to ring, an unforeseen tragedy befalls Rupert, turning Langston Hall upside down.

Equally entrapped by societal expectations and her burgeoning feelings,

Miss Stronghold also finds herself at a crossroads. With the stability of Langston Hall and the future of its inhabitants uncertain, will Edmund and Abigail confront the dictates of their class and follow their hearts, or will they forsake personal happiness for the sake of tradition and duty?

This Regency romance weaves a compelling story of love, loss, and the choices that define us.

The Thunderbolt Series - Book 1

Ebook & Paperback

one starry night

FATE HAS JOINED THEM TOGETHER, WILL REVENGE OR LOVE BE NEXT?

Miss Charlotte Elkins was the mistress of the Marquess of Harcourt. She had been exclusively his for the past several years. She would have stood by him forever if he hadn't taken a wife without warning. On one starry night, Charlotte sees the Marquess with his wife and is so distraught, runs into the arms of a man with a dangerous past.

Mr. Silas St. Clair was a scandalous rogue. Many ladies had fallen into his trap. Seeing his favorite suddenly wed sends him into a tailspin and into the arms of his competitors mistress.

Read *One Starry Night*, a Standalone Regency Novella!

Available in
ebook & paperback

service daughter series

YOUR NEXT SERIES

HARDSHIP SHOULDN'T HAVE TO BE SUCH AN UPHILL BATTLE

Meet Louisa, Caroline & Hannah

Three daughters born into service. Each with their own story to tell and happily ever after. Simple, ordinary and untitled, unnoticed by the wealthy, struggling with how to survive, how to obtain joy...much less a husband.

ALL LOUISA WANTED WAS TO BE USEFUL...

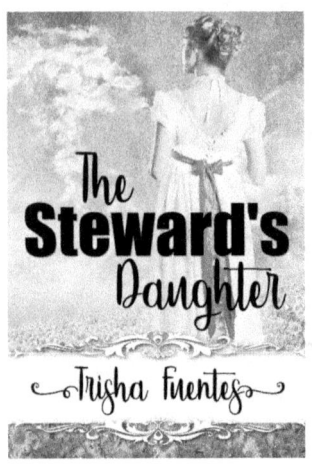

The only child of Mr. Ralph Hadley, Land Steward to the Earl of Monbossom, Miss Louisa Hadley lives in a small cottage on the Monbossom estate with her father. When she accidentally breaks her foot after dismounting a horse she is forced to stay in the main house while her father tends to the Earl abroad. With the family now responsible for Louisa's well-being, the classes have reversed as Louisa is constantly scorned by her friends in service. Her circumstances take a more dramatic turn when she stumbles upon the Earl of Monbossom while saving a duckling.

When did he return from France? And who knew his eyes were so blue?

Book 1
Ebook & Paperback

CAN A KITCHEN MAID FIND TRUE HAPPINESS?

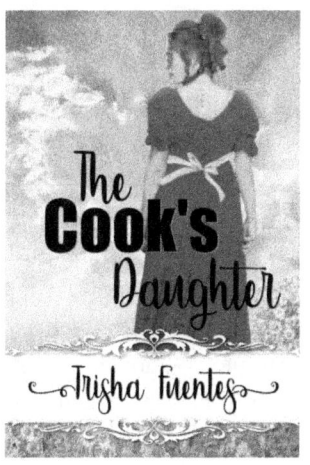

Miss Caroline Bates began working in the kitchen with her mother when she was twelve. Caroline grew up with the children of Wellsbury Hall, and watched Lord Gretner's eldest son, Alfred court several noblewomen until one day he finds Caroline practically naked in a nearby moor river.

Is Caroline ruined for all eternity or does she use this mischance to her advantage?

Book 2
Ebook & Paperback

WHICH PATH TO FOLLOW?

The only daughter of a curator of St. Anne's Church, Miss Hannah Pickering grew up knowing she was going to become a nun until she is introduced to one of her father's parishioners. Tempted by the handsome widower who attends her father's church, Hannah is suddenly forced to make a worrisome decision.

Book 3
Ebook & Paperback

about trisha

Hey, it's Trish...

I'm a Romance Author of 40+ books, plus a Publishing House Owner of 50+ Pen Name Authors.

I've been writing romance with a whole lot of heat lately. I love to write fun, fast romances with witty leading ladies getting that gorgeous, sexy, yet lovable guy that doesn't take months to finish. Happily Ever After with a little bit of love angst in between. Whether you yearn for Historical or Modern, I always have a story for you!

Rejoice, Romance Reader...

For upcoming releases, book news, and other goodies,

subscribe to my Newsletter!
https://bit.ly/49BR3UB

- instagram.com/authortrish
- amazon.com/Trisha-Fuentes/e/B002BME1MI
- facebook.com/booksbyTrish
- youtube.com/theardentartist

also by trisha fuentes

❋ Modern Romance ❋

A Sacrifice Play

Faded Dreams

Never Say Forever

❋ Historical ❋

The Anzan Heir

Magnet & Steele

The Relentless Rogue

One Starry Night

In The Moonlight With You

Captivating the Captain

The Merry Widow

Unrequited Love

The Summer Romance of the Duke

A Dare Maid in Vain

❋ Series ❋

HOLLINGER

Dare To Love - Book 1

A Matchless Match - Book 2

Arrogance & Conceit - Book 3

Impropriety - Book 4

SERVICE·DAUGHTER
The Steward's Daughter - Book 1
The Cook's Daughter - Book 2
The Curator's Daughter - Book 3

THUNDERBOLT
The Surprise Heir - Book 1
A Dance of Deception - Book 2
Win the Heart of a Duchess- Book 3

OBSESSION
Unsuitable Obsession - Part One
Broken Obsession - Part Two

ESCAPE
Swept Away - Book 1
Fire & Rescue - Book 2
The Domain King - Book 3

AGE·GAP·ROMANCE
Whispers of Yesterday - Book 1
His Encore, Her Ecstasy - Book 2
Against the Wind - Book 3

SERIAL·ROMANCE
The Rekindled Flame - Book 1

The Power of Two - Book 2
Facing the Past - Book 3
Taking a Chance - Book 4
Choosing the Future - Book 5

✽

➥**Full Paperback**

https://bit.ly/3XbNK2e

www.ingramcontent.com/pod-product-compliance
Lightning Source LLC
LaVergne TN
LVHW010325070526
838199LV00065B/5662